BEARSKIN TO HOLLY FORK

Bearskin to Holly Fork

Stories from Appalachia

Bob Sloan

Wind Publications
2003

First Edition

International Standard Book Number 1-893239-21-7
Library of Congress Control Number: 2003106240

A version of some of these stories have appeared in various quarterlies and "little" magazines. I am immensely grateful to their editors for having given space and attention to my work.

Appalachian Heritage — "Junior Blevins" and "Finding the Gate"
Buffalo Spree — "Willard's Got a Problem" & "A Good Man to Talk With"
Echoes — "Troops"
Hob-Nob — "Three Towsacks of Grapefruit: a Kentucky Memory of the Great Depression"
Just a Moment — "Jesse's Becky"
M - The Magazine of the Mountains — "Symbiosis"
Mountain Laurel — "Finding the Gate"
Potpourri — "The Whole Story," "Fire, and Stella," & "Obligation"
Sidewalks — "A Ride Across Open Water"
Wind Magazine — "The Window"

Front cover photo by Julie Sloan
Rear cover author's photo by Marcus Brown

Acknowledgments

The support, encouragement and assistance of a host of people have allowed me to live every writer's fantasy, to hold a copy of a book and say, "*I* wrote this."

Once upon a very long time ago, a special librarian opened up the world of books for a surly, smart-mouthed kid, encouraged him to read anything that caught his interest, then question what he read, to write, to think. I was the kid. A wonderful woman—and fellow writer—named Jeanne Burr was the librarian. Thank you Jeanne.

Joy Campbell is the best kid sister in the world, and her faith in me has been more important than she knows. She believes this is the first of several books that will bear my name as "author." If she's right, in no small part it's because of her constant, consistent encouragement.

John Eddy, my great and good friend for over thirty years, knew I was a writer before I did. After college, the business of writing stories and getting them into print seemed so daunting—and unlikely—that I gave it up entirely. For a decade and a half I wrote nothing more complicated than long letters to friends. Over the years, conversations with John *always* ended with his question, "You writing anything?" His gentle nagging ultimately drove me to buy my first word processor and get back in the game. Thanks, John, for thirty years of company, conversation, and caring.

My wife Julie is smarter than me, has more common sense and is a masterful critic, editor, and proofreader. I'd no more submit a story without asking her to read it first than I'd hand-write a manuscript. Julie makes me a better writer, and a better man than I'd ever be without her. She is my partner in all things, my best friend, and the love of my life. Julie's company beats the hell out of time spent with anyone else on this earth. I am indebted to her on levels beyond counting. Thanks, love.

Charlie Hughes is a world-class poet. Look for his work, and go hear him read it if you get a chance. Not only does he bring fine lyrical writing into the world, he is the guiding light behind Wind Publications, which made this book. Thank you, Charlie. I'm not the best writer you've published, but I suspect I'm the most grateful.

And for deciding to read these stories, thank *you,* whoever you are. All writers are only responding to the age-old plea, "Tell me a story." That you would choose to pay attention to mine is an honor, and it is high privilege to tell you the stories which follow.

For my mother
Marjorie Martt Sloan
(1926-1998)
A far better story-teller than I

CONTENTS

Introduction

The whole Appalachian community of Midland, Kentucky, comes to life in this fine debut collection of tough, true stories, each one hard and dark as a lump of coal. Bob Sloan's straight, plain prose style is perfectly suited to his characters and their lives. They include, among others: a hallucinating veteran, a mandolin player who has finally come to the "bad end" everybody has been predicting for him all along, carpenters, marijuana growers, millworkers, bootleggers, "Navy retreads," patient wives and wild women, miners and loggers.

Their stories are about work and family and hard times, and how a man can find release from these things upon occasion, such as Tommy Sewell, a lumberyard owner who is "fixing to throw his life away for a little bit of strange." In one of my favorites, an unemployed logger gets into a lot of trouble due to a woman he meets in "mad class"—his court-mandated anger management group held in a trailer behind the mental health clinic. Here he describes her:

> Mary Parton's beautiful is what she is.
> Every time she moved I thought of hawks in
> high summer, soaring clean and easy, beautiful without ever thinking what they look like.
> Outside the Doc's trailer, that's how she
> strolled over to me, graceful as a hawk.
> Gimme a ride home? she asked.

In "A Good Man to Talk With," our teenaged narrator tells us that the funeral preacher talked about "what he thought Paul was . . . But he never mentioned guitars or mandolins, and he didn't say anything about brown pint bottles. He didn't say anything about being a good man to talk with . . . He didn't talk about Paul at all."

The themes of some stories are surprising. In "Fire, and Stella," a barn burning illuminates adultery. A runaway wife and a dead baby figure in "A Ride Across Open Water;" while a mother's old boyfriend shows up at her funeral in "Junior Blevins"—much to her son's consternation. An old friendship is put to the ultimate test in "Obligation."

It often comes down to people who have options and people who don't. In "Finding the Gate," an old woman in a nursing home muses that, "The young nurses who work in this place believe in options, in free choice. I hear them often, earnest and convinced, assuring one another every woman has opportunities beyond only doing what men want. Perhaps I had opportunities too, and settled on the wrong ones. But looking back, it seems to me things just happened." To her, "these Kentucky mountains seemed to be a . . . fence so high we could neither cross nor see beyond it." She wanted a gate—a way out—but "by the time I was 25 I had four daughters, and felt old." Paradoxically, her wild, wandering son proved to be "the saving" of her.

If they arrive at all in Midland, options come mostly through love. When Roy Carter's old friend Johnny Ellis turns up again like a bad penny, Roy shares an insight with his wife: "We're not a whole lot different, Johnny and me." But Roy has Janine; they've been together since age 17. "You were MY reason. You wouldn't stand for it, and I wanted things to work out for us. . . . Johnny never in this life had nothing at all to care about working out."

Whether things work out for his characters or not, realist Bob Sloan makes us care about them all, writing in plain honest prose without a trace of sentimentality.

Welcome to Midland.

— Lee Smith

THE WINDOW

A small, distant sound—the hollow resonance of tires rolling over gravel—stops Roy Carter where he stands. His fingers are wrapped around the screen door latch, and in another ten seconds he'd have been in the house. But wondering who's driving up the hill after ten o'clock of a Friday evening is enough to settle Roy back into the porch glider.

He wonders if an ambulance is fighting the steep grade from the highway. Elmer and Rosie Glover live farther down the road. Elmer's got heart trouble and Rosie's so frail it's over six months since anybody saw her in town. More than a few people assume she's died. There's no siren though, no chaos of flashing red beacons, just headlights.

Their full glare sweeps across the porch as a vehicle pulls into Roy's driveway. When the lights go out there's a black hole of an after-image in Roy's vision. He recognizes the shape of a Ford pickup, but the driver stands in indistinct darkness.

At the words "Hey, buddy," spoken out of the night, Roy relaxes. He's surprised how much he tensed up, listening to the truck's approach.

"Hey yourself," he answers, and Johnny Ellis moves through light spilling from the living room windows. Johnny climbs the porch steps, shifts a chair so it points toward Roy, then folds his long angular self into it. "Wasn't sure if you'd be up or not."

Roy smells whiskey all the way across the porch. "Want a beer?"

Johnny shakes his head. "Nah. Want a taste of this?"

3

Roy's not sure where the pint bottle comes from. It wasn't in Johnny's hand when he climbed the steps. Roy studies the bottle a moment before leaning forward to take it. Hard liquor can put him in a mean state of mind; Roy mostly gave it up a long time ago. He hasn't had a dozen shots of whiskey in four or five years.

Roy doesn't bother looking at the label as he lifts the bottle, tilts it and lets cheap bourbon flow to the core of his being. Closing his eyes, he focuses on the sweet after-taste, the ebb of the sharp burn in his belly to friendly warmth. If he weren't afraid of whiskey, Roy'd drink it every night.

Johnny takes a much longer swallow, and a deep breath behind it. "I figure you had something to do with me getting hired on with Charlie Sturgill," he says. "Might be a little late, but I wanted to tell you I appreciate it."

"Didn't do much," Roy says.

In fact, he had not a thing to do with Johnny Ellis getting a job with Charlie.

Not that it matters now.

Ten hours ago, right before the Friday noon break, Johnny got fired.

Or quit.

Or something.

Roy isn't sure what to call it.

Johnny asks, "You won't get in any trouble over what happened will you?"

As Roy shakes his head, the light shifts as Janine comes to stand in the doorway, arms folded to keep her housecoat closed. "You coming to bed?" she asks. Johnny clears his throat, and Roy imagines the blush spreading across his wife's face.

"I didn't know there was anybody else here," Janine says. She comes outside, settles into the glider beside Roy, and scowls subtle disapproval. The change in Janine's expression would be missed by most people, but Roy sees it. Any wife would frown, finding her husband with Johnny Ellis.

"You remember Johnny," Roy says to Janine. "I told you about him coming to work with us."

4

A month ago, Charlie Sturgill, the contractor who's been Roy's boss for ten years, told the crew a new guy was coming to work with them soon. When Charlie asked if any of them knew Johnny Ellis, Roy admitted they'd gone to school together. That's all he said, that they'd gone to the same school.

Truth is Roy and Johnny used to be best friends.

But that was a long time ago.

Charlie partnered them up until Johnny learned the job's routine. Working together was the first time Roy and Johnny talked in better than ten years. Sitting on Roy's darkened porch is the first time they've seen one another outside the job.

When Johnny offers the bottle again, Roy hesitates, not sure how Janine will act if she sees him drinking whiskey. He takes the bourbon anyway, pretends he doesn't notice her grimace.

"Nice house," Johnny says, after the bottle's in his hand again.

Roy feels better when the pint disappears back to wherever it came from. "Built it right after we got married."

If Johnny's disappointed at not being asked inside for a tour, it doesn't show. "Man oh man," he murmurs as wind carries a redolence of fresh mown grass to the porch. "That is a sweet smell of an evening."

"Matt Sparks was cutting hay till just a little while ago," Roy says. "You could hear his tractor on the other side of the hill way after dark."

"Maridell Sparks's daddy?" Johnny breathes deep, like he's hungry for the smell of cut hay.

Where Johnny's been, a man would miss hay. And a lot of other things besides.

"Who'd Maridell marry anyway?"

Roy lifts his legs, props them on the porch rail. "I don't reckon I ever heard. She moved to Louisville, and after that I don't know. Seen her in town a couple years ago, visiting."

"She still a good looking thing?" Johnny asks.

Roy thinks it's a rude question to put to a married man, with his wife sitting right there. "She hasn't changed a whole lot," he offers, remembering Maridell was someone Johnny chased around with in the old days.

Johnny takes another long breath. "One time I stood in a barn where a thousand pounds of stuff was hanging, just like tobacco curing. It didn't smell a whole lot different than hay." He empties his lungs in a loud sigh. "But the other, that was the smell of big money."

A couple of weeks before coming to work for Charlie Sturgill, Johnny Ellis walked out of LaGrange Prison after seven years of hard time lock-up. Other people in the county have been arrested for growing pot, but Roy never knew any of them. He can't really say he knows Johnny Ellis, but he did, once upon a time.

Thirty seconds of silence stretch all the way to discomfort. Roy turns toward Janine, tells her, "Johnny's the reason I'm a carpenter."

Johnny laughs. "How you figure that, hoss?"

Roy directs his answer to Janine. "Back when we were kids, me and Johnny were friends. By the time we got to be fifteen I was failing school and figured I'd put one more year in and quit."

Roy explains how Johnny talked him into changing from college prep stuff to vocational classes. Roy's mother pitched a conniption fit, but he was a whole lot happier. Instead of being mystified by algebra questions that didn't make sense, he worked shop math problems that did. In a woodworking class Roy discovered tools filled his hands naturally, as though he'd been handling them from birth, and found he liked building things. The class carried him into carpentry and construction.

"If you hadn't said I belonged in trade school I don't know what would have happened to me," Roy says at the end, turning to face Johnny again.

"What did *you* do after high school?" Janine's question sounds accusatory.

There's not enough light from the windows for Roy to tell if Johnny's smile is the hard grin he aims at people at work who ask about prison. Johnny never answers their questions, and nobody voices them twice.

"Berea College," Johnny says. "Majored in pot and parties. Come home and had a few good years."

Johnny shifts in the rocking chair, the whiskey bottle comes out again, and he takes a long hit. He laughs, but not like anything's funny. "Maybe I ought to've gone to trade school too. Wound up in the same place as Roy, and *he* didn't have to move all the way to Berea to get there."

"How do you like working for Charlie?" Janine asks.

"Liked it fine till that fat fuck Fraley got on my ass today." Johnny laughs again, and this time something *is* funny. "Now I got to find another job."

Janine falls quiet, and Roy wonders if it's because of the rough language or a sense she may've taken the talk into a place it ought not to have gone. In a moment she gets up and goes in the house, rigid with righteous offense, and Roy figures it's because of the language.

"Sorry, man," Johnny says. "Sometimes I forget there's women around."

Roy lifts a dismissive hand at the apology. It's not like his wife heard any words she didn't already know. "Call Delbert up tomorrow or Sunday," he tells Johnny after the screen door slaps shut behind Janine. "Maybe he'll get over what happened."

Roy knows he's voicing a lie.

Delbert Fraley's their foreman, and that afternoon, for a few seconds Johnny put fear into Delbert's eyes, easy to read as words on a billboard. Nobody on the crew missed it. Their knowing Delbert was afraid means Johnny's not coming back to work. Delbert can't keep a man who scares him on the crew.

Johnny puts the whiskey away. Roy still can't tell where the bottle goes. "Maybe if I hadn't slung that hammer."

"You're lucky it missed Delbert's head," Roy tells him.

Johnny stands up, and Roy notices he puts a hand on the porch rail to steady himself. "Gotta go," he says. "Things to see, people to do, stuff like that."

The door opens and Janine comes back outside. Roy's surprised she'd so obviously eavesdrop at the open window, then come onto

7

the porch like she might have to stop Roy from driving off into the night with a drunk ex-convict.

Johnny smiles at her. "'Scuse my language a while ago."

Janine doesn't say anything, just stands by the door, watching.

"You okay to drive?" Roy asks. "I can take you anywhere you need to go."

Johnny shakes his head. "I don't reckon there's a place in Tyler County I can't drive to blindfolded." He moves to the first porch step. "And drunk besides."

Once on the ground, Johnny reaches for the hidden bourbon. "You're right though. I had enough of this." He places the bottle on the porch rail like he's afraid it might jump off, then goes to his truck, his pace the deliberate march of the very intoxicated.

Roy watches the pickup back out of the driveway. Lights don't come on until Johnny's found first gear and started off the hill. Roy hopes the state police aren't setting up checkpoints. He's pretty sure people just out of prison aren't allowed to drink, and anybody who gets within three yards of Johnny Ellis will know he spent the evening looking for the bottom of a whiskey bottle.

Roy reaches for the pint, still warm from wherever it was hidden. "Don't get started," he warns Janine. Since he stopped making church more than one Sunday in three Janine's quick to ride him about drinking. He holds the bottle up to the light. It's about a quarter full.

"Shouldn't have let him drive off like that," Janine mutters.

Roy figures she's talking to herself as much as to him. "Couldn't have stopped him."

"How come he threw a hammer at Delbert?" she asks.

"He didn't throw it *at* him," Roy says. "They were arguing and Johnny kind of tossed it into the air."

"What were they arguing over?" Janine presses.

"A window," Roy tells her. "Johnny got himself fired over a little girl's window."

Then he tells Janine what happened.

Before the noon break, Delbert Fraley left to make sure the lumber yard would deliver roof trusses that afternoon. If the crew didn't have trusses waiting to be set Monday morning, they'd all have an unpaid day off.

After the foreman drove away the half dozen men in the house leaned on walls and talked weekend plans. The married ones argued about whether it was too hot to go fishing. Single men talked about beer joints and the women they'd find there.

Thirty, forty minutes after Delbert left, a familiar blue Dodge mini-van pulled onto the job site. Ruthie Harrison, half of the couple whose house they were building, had come one more time to see their progress. From the day the foundation was laid on her new house, Ruthie's shown up maybe once a week. Nobody minds.

Roy tells Janine home-owners-to-be are most of the time a nuisance. They have less than a glimmer of a notion how a house is put together, and when they're not asking stupid questions, they stand where they're most in the way.

Ruthie's different.

She usually comes late in the day, after picking her three kids up from day care. The kids play in the woods behind the new house, and Ruthie doesn't come inside unless she has a plate of cookies or a cake for the crew. She does that a lot, brings something she's baked. Not even Delbert Fraley minds Ruthie Harrison coming around.

This time she showed up around ten thirty. With the crew goofing off the job was quiet. Roy tells Janine the quiet is probably why Ruthie left her car, walked into what will be her living room, and commenced a slow dreamy stroll through the skeleton of her house.

He doesn't say anything about every man on the crew watching Ruthie, trying not to be obvious about looking. She's the kind of trim, slim head turner who wouldn't be out of place in one of those magazines under the counter at the Readi-Mart. When she's around it's easy to think about seeing her naked like the women in those slick pages. Wrapped up in imagining her house, Ruthie acted like she didn't care who watched her, or how closely.

Anytime the crew kicks back, Johnny Ellis goes off by himself, finds a place to lean against a wall stud, and reads. He always has a

9

book in the back pocket of his jeans. Ruthie Harrison, wandering through her daydream, found him in a back bedroom. That's how she wound up speaking to Johnny, instead of somebody who would have told her it was too late to change the window.

When Roy realized Ruthie and Johnny'd been talking a whole lot longer than it takes to say "Hello," or "How's it going?" he moved close enough to listen. Roy doesn't tell his wife he was a little worried about what a man seven years in prison might say to Ruthie Harrison.

He listened as Ruthie explained the room she and Johnny were in would be her five-year-old daughter's bedroom. Then Johnny Ellis talked about *his* daughter, said she was nine and he sure did understand how happy Ruthie's little girl would be to have her own room.

Roy vaguely remembers Johnny being married for a while to one of the Simpson sisters. Renee, he thinks it was. Roy's pretty sure they're divorced.

Janine interrupts, says Johnny Ellis wasn't married to Renee Simpson, it was Renee's sister Robin, but that Roy's right about the divorce. Not long before Johnny went to prison Robin married a guy in the Navy and moved to San Diego.

Roy nods and goes back to the story of what happened that afternoon.

Johnny didn't talk to Ruthie Harrison like he had an ex-wife and daughter half a continent away. He made it sound like his family was right there in Tyler County, and he'd see them soon as he got off work. Roy tells Janine that was why he didn't interfere. He didn't know if he'd be able to look Johnny in the eye, interrupting such a whopper of a lie.

Ruthie went to stand in front of a window facing the woods. It wasn't a real window yet, just the shape of one, outlined by raw lumber and Celotex. Ruthie said her girl Casey would spend a lot of time perched on a chair, looking outside. After a while she wondered if the window could be lowered, if it could be fixed so a small child could see outside without climbing onto something.

10

Roy couldn't believe it when Johnny said he'd change the window himself, right then and there if Ruthie wanted to stay and watch.

It didn't take as much as twenty minutes to modify the wall so the window was a couple feet lower, even with Roy trying to talk him out of what he was doing. Roy kept talking while Johnny built a new header out of an eight-foot two-by-ten, cut new jacks and cripples from a couple of studs to reframe the space.

Talking low enough Ruthie Harrison wouldn't hear, Roy reminded Johnny that Delbert Fraley would pitch a fit, and not just over wasting lumber. There were four other windows in the wall. Dropping one of them two feet would throw the look of the whole house off.

Roy tells Janine that Johnny said he wasn't worried about Fraley getting mad.

But that wasn't what Johnny said, or how he said it.

What he really said was "*Fuck* Delbert Fraley. If a person wants to do something nice for their little girl, they ought to do it. This ain't Delbert Fraley's house, it's *her* house and I'm just fixing a window the way she wants it."

And Johnny said "Fucking people so fucking tight-assed about fucking windows lining up oughta find something else to fucking bitch about."

The more he talked about it the more excited Johnny got. The madder he got, really, so Roy backed off. "You don't crowd a man who's pissed off and holding a framing hammer," he tells Janine.

Nobody on the crew said a word, but there wasn't a pair of eyes in that shell of a house not watching Johnny Ellis storm through the business of reframing the little girl's window. Ruthie Harrison's eyes were happy and excited, and the crew was happy in a whole other way. There'd be a show when Delbert Fraley saw what Johnny had done. Moving the window was just the first act, and the crew was looking forward to the rest.

Roy didn't want to see any kind of a show. Johnny was making trouble for himself, for no good reason, like he always had. Watch-

11

ing him nail the header and jacks in place Roy remembered things he hadn't thought about in years.

How Johnny one time gave the finger to Paulie Conley, on a day they'd skipped school to fish the Weaver Hole. Paulie was a deputy sheriff, looking for shade where he could park his cruiser for an afternoon nap. He'd have left them alone if Johnny hadn't raised his right arm straight up in the air, middle digit extended, grinning like a monkey. Paulie chased them for an hour.

The deputy must have weighed more than three hundred pounds, and the fat man hasn't been born who can catch two thirteen year olds, even with them carrying rods and reels and a tackle box. They got away, but it didn't matter. The deputy knew who they were, and went to both their houses and told their folks the boys were truant.

Watching Johnny swing his hammer—swing it a whole lot harder than he needed to—Roy remembered a morning Johnny called Mrs. Reed, their history teacher, a bitch right to her face, and got himself kicked out of school for three days.

There was another time in high school, right before Roy changed to vo-tech classes. Walking out of a boys' restroom after an illicit cigarette, Johnny emptied a chest full of smoke in the face of the assistant principal everybody called "Hose Nose."

Half a dozen events slipped into Roy's consciousness as he watched Johnny with the window, things he hadn't thought about in forever, all of them about Johnny making trouble for himself.

When Johnny was done reworking the little girl's window, Ruthie hollered five year old Casey out of the woods and had her stand there to show it was just at the right height for a child to look into the trees.

Then Ruthie Harrison did something that surprised all of them: she hugged Johnny, right in front of the little girl. It wasn't an out of place hug, not even close to what the single men would get at a bar that night, after slow dancing with some saloon cutie, but still. There wasn't any light showing between them for a second or two.

Everybody took turns trading glances over that hug while Ruthie herded the kids into her minivan and drove off. The dust hadn't yet settled from her leaving when they heard Delbert Fraley's old Chevy rumbling down the county road outside the housing development. Delbert's pickup needed a new muffler, and its engine roar carried half a mile.

By the time the foreman got his Chevy parked a pair of saws were running, and anyone who wasn't sawing found a place that needed a nail or two, fire blocks to put in place, whatever would keep their hands busy. All the work happened in places where it was easy to watch Delbert stalk across the littered yard and pause, take a long look at the wall where one window was two feet lower than when he'd left for town.

Johnny Ellis wasn't a bit interested in watching Delbert. He stood where Ruthie'd found him, leaned up against his wall, his book open like he might get in another few pages before the foreman cleaned his clock.

Delbert Fraley stomped into the house and didn't look at anybody except Johnny, and stopped right in front of him. When the foreman put a hand out, like he was going to snatch the book away, Johnny aimed a gaze over the pages and Delbert's hand stopped in mid-air.

"What in the merry hell is *that*?" Delbert demanded, pointing at the lowered hole in the wall.

His voice calm and easy, like he was explaining something to an idiot child instead of a pissed off foreman who outweighed him by seventy pounds, Johnny told Delbert that Ruthie had wanted the window lowered for her little girl. And never dropped his book even an inch.

Roy tells Janine if Delbert Fraley looked at *him* the way he looked at Johnny Ellis, he'd want a whole lot more than a book to hold, but Johnny stood there like he couldn't wait for Delbert to hush so he could get back to an interesting part.

Delbert did a lot of shouting and carrying on, without crowding any closer to Johnny. He said when Charlie Sturgill by God heard about that window foolishness, Johnny'd be looking for a new job, and it wouldn't surprise Delbert a bit if Charlie docked whatever pay Johnny had coming, for the lumber he'd wasted.

Johnny just stood there and stared into the foreman's eyes, and after a while the fear came onto Delbert. His eyes began to shift, looking anywhere but Johnny's face. The pace and a half between the two made it obvious to the crew that Delbert was afraid of crowding the smaller man.

The foreman would have problems for a while as others tested to see if they could put the same furtive look in Delbert's eyes. And none of them had known Delbert couldn't fire them, that firing was a decision reserved for Charlie Sturgill.

The foreman didn't stop talking so much as he seemed to run out of heat and words. He stood there quiet for a while, like he was reaching down inside himself for something else to say and not finding anything.

"You done?" Johnny asked when Delbert was quiet for maybe ten seconds.

"Fuck you, Ellis," Delbert said. "I'm gonna have your job."

"Keep your silly-ass job," Johnny told him in that smooth voice.

Walking away, Johnny pulled the framing hammer from his tool belt and heaved it into the air. If the roof had been in place the tool would have bounced back down among the crew, but it sailed thirty, thirty-five feet above the open house before starting down.

Delbert Fraley watched the hammer at the top of its arc like he was the only one there who didn't know it was about to split his head wide open. At the last second the foreman jerked forward a single step, and the tool fell to the plywood subfloor behind him, bounced twice, and was still.

Roy tells Janine it wasn't till he let his breath out he realized how long he'd been holding it, and it sounded like some other people did the same thing.

"Then what happened?" Janine asks.

"Not much." Roy stretches his legs out, but slouching on the glider is uncomfortable, and he straightens himself after a few seconds. "Johnny drove off and the rest of us set down and ate our dinner. Then we went back to work." Roy uncaps the pint bottle and swallows what's left of the bourbon.

14

"Can he get his job back?" Janine looks away as Roy drinks the whiskey, but doesn't say anything.

"I don't think so," Roy says.

"Too bad."

Roy doesn't like the sound of Janine's voice. It's like she doesn't think it's too bad at all, and he feels himself get angry. "Johnny's a good guy."

"Sounds a little crazy to me."

"He ain't no more crazy than I am."

Roy lifts his arm, pitches the bourbon bottle overhand into the yard, hard as he can throw it. It bounces across the grass a few times without breaking. He'll have to go pick the bottle up before he goes to bed, but throwing it felt good. "There's not a lot of difference between Johnny and me."

Janine flinches when Roy throws the bottle, but then she snickers. "You're not a *thing* like Johnny Ellis."

Roy wishes the six pack of MGD in the refrigerator was close enough he could stick out his hand and find a cold beer to grip. "When Johnny started growing dope he asked me to help him."

Janine grins like she's waiting for a punch line to a joke, and when there isn't one, moves to lean against the porch rail so she's looking straight at Roy. "You never told me that."

"He almost talked me into it," Roy admits. "That was when we were wanting to build this house. I figured a year or two with Johnny and I could almost have it paid off, instead of owing the bank."

Tired of wishing the beer was closer, Roy gets up, stomps into the house, and carries the six pack to the porch. The cans are already sweating as he pops the first top. "If I'd've done it Johnny might not have got caught."

"How's that?" Janine doesn't look at the beer, keeps her gaze fixed on Roy's face. He can almost feel the intensity of her stare, faint heat on his skin.

"It was because of that old four wheel drive Dodge I had when we got married that Johnny asked me. He had him a pot patch the

15

hell and gone off in the National Forest, at the end of an old logging road too rough for whatever he was driving back then."

Roy lifts the beer and empties half the can in a single draw. "The Dodge could take him right where he needed to go, but since all he had was some old car no good for driving in the woods he had to fetch and carry things half a mile. That's how he got caught, toting five gallon buckets of water to those plants. Somebody noticed what he was doing and turned him in."

When Roy sighs, the breath leaving his body carries away some of the anger—or whatever it is—churning his belly. He empties the beer, snaps open another, past caring what Janine thinks about drinking. "We're not a whole lot different, Johnny and me," he says.

Roy sits quiet for a while, not sure what he wants to say to his wife, let alone how to say it.

The first time he told Janine he loved her, they were seventeen, wrestling around in his old Dodge truck, parked on a Forest Service fire trail. After he muttered the words against her feverish neck, Janine took her blouse off. Roy did love her, as far as a teenaged boy can love anyone, but he's not sure he would have said the words, except for the blouse.

They've been together a long time, and Roy can't imagine a life without Janine, knows he's a better man for having her with him. But words like "love" are no easier to say out loud than when Roy and Janine were just beginning.

"Renee, Robin, whatever his wife's name was, she was running around on him. Johnny didn't have any reason not to grow dope and make big money for a while." Roy looks at Janine a long time. "You were *my* reason. You wouldn't stand for it, and I wanted things to work out for us."

Roy shakes his head, pissed at the unfairness of it all. Pissed at something anyway. "Johnny never in this life had nothing at all to care about working out."

"Well." Janine stands away from the porch rail, puts a hand on Roy's shoulder and squeezes. "People like that can be dangerous to be around, don't you think?"

Roy opens a third beer. The alcohol buzz reaching from his head all the way to his legs feels good. He hears Janine go into the house, and knows he'll follow before too much longer. She'll be in their bed, and they probably won't make love because Janine hates the smell of beer.

But she'll lay her head on his shoulder, and they'll slip off to sleep, still touching.

Tomorrow Roy will call Charlie Sturgill, try and talk the contractor into giving Johnny's job back to him. It might mean Delbert Fraley quitting, but maybe Charlie'll go along with it.

Maybe.

One more beer and Roy will go to bed.

But first he'll walk out and pick up that empty whiskey bottle.

A Good Man to Talk with

I was on top of the shed nailing shingles and saw the sheriff's car turn off the highway at the foot of the hill. Luke was on the ground behind the shed and couldn't see it, but I didn't say anything. Whenever they arrested Paul Rafferty the police sent a man out to fetch Luke to town so he could post his son's bond. I don't reckon the old man ever owned a car. I went on laying down shingles and nailing them, watching Luke out of the corner of my eye.

Luke saw the car when the deputy parked by the house, and a tight expression settled over his face. Without looking at me he said, "You get on down now boy. I reckon we're through for the day."

"I can finish by myself, Mr. Rafferty," I said. I didn't want to wait because the next day was Sunday. Luke wouldn't work on Sundays, and unless the shingles got nailed on while I was already there, I'd have to spend my next Saturday doing it.

"No," Luke insisted. "You get on down. We'll finish next week."

I was sixteen then, and Luke would hire me to work around his place some weekends, jobs that meant heavy lifting or climbing, things he was too tired and worn out for. He always seemed satisfied with my work but insisted on watching, as though he didn't trust me even to roof a shed without his supervision. I climbed down to put the hammer and nails in the building and he said "Come on to the house and I'll pay what I owe."

I told him, "I can wait for the money." I didn't want to go with him to hear what Paul had been up to.

"No, you come on up to the house," the old man insisted. "I'll pay what I owe and then I'll have to go to town." As I followed his stooped shoulders Luke added, "I always pay what I owe, boy. I never owed airy man if I could he'p it."

The deputy was waiting by the porch. "Something bad happened, Mr. Rafferty," he said, and from his voice I knew this time it was different.

"I know." Luke's voice was tired and he seemed to stare through the deputy. "What's my boy done?" Luke sighed and turned his eyes back in the direction of the shed. "What's he cost me this time?"

"Mr. Rafferty, maybe you better set down or something." The deputy looked at me like he wanted some help, and I wished I'd gone on home. Then, with a rush, rolling words from his mouth as though they had a bad taste he said, "Mr. Rafferty, Paul's dead. Sam Stevens shot him and he's dead. I'm sorry."

Luke's face was the color of a ripe tomato as he fell over.

"Oh my God," the deputy said, reaching to catch him, but the old man hit the ground anyway, hard. We carried Luke into the house and laid him on the couch. "He got a phone?" the deputy asked, out of breath. When I shook my head he ran out to his car and used the radio to call an ambulance.

There was a frightened, wild look in the deputy's eyes when he came back inside. "I never thought this would happen," he said, and it was like he was asking for something.

"You couldn't help it," I told him. I looked down at Luke and thought he was gone till I saw the eyelids flutter.

Midland Hospital is a long way off, and by the time the ambulance got there Luke was sitting up. He sat shaking his head, twisting his wrinkled brown hands together, and when the medical people wanted to take him to the hospital he said he wasn't going anyplace.

"Is there anyone could stay with him for a while?" the deputy asked.

"My folks live at the foot of this hill," I told him. "My mother could come."

So the deputy went in his car and brought my mother to Luke's. She asked for Dr. Caudill to be sent out from town and then she said to me, "Go on home. When your daddy gets there you tell him where I am."

I rode down in the sheriff's car, and then I was alone at our place. I went into my bedroom and got the pack of cigarettes my folks weren't supposed to know about. I hadn't smoked since walking to Luke's early in the morning, and it was good to sit on the porch and light up. I tried to think of Paul Rafferty dead, and couldn't.

Paul wasn't yet thirty, and he was the first person I'd known who was young and died. With old people it was different. Death seemed to take them slowly, like a cat with a cornered mouse, coming very close before the final strike. Their dying was thought about so often, it was easier to know an old man was dead than a young one.

As I smoked I thought of how Paul Rafferty had been the first adult to treat me like a man. When he came home from the army I was thirteen, and had nearly my full growth. I wanted to be treated like the man I felt inside, but to my folks and others who'd known me all my life I was still "Tommy," and they spoke to me in the same tones they used when I was seven and eight and nine.

Paul was different. He didn't talk at me but to me, and listened as carefully to what I said as he did to my father. He wanted to know what I thought about things, and if he didn't agree we talked about our differences like men. He called me "Tom." He was all right, Paul was.

When my father came home from the lumber yard I didn't hear the car drive up, didn't know he was there till he asked, "When did you start smoking?"

"About a year ago," I answered, surprised to find him so close without my knowing.

"A year. A long time." He looked at the smoldering Camel in my hand and said, "Hadn't you ought to at least smoke one with a filter?"

"These are okay," I said.

Paul always told me, "If you ain't smoking Camels you're trying to quit."

My father sat on the edge of the porch, leaning against one of the posts as he unlaced his heavy work boots. "Where's your mother?" he asked when he straightened.

"Up to Luke's. Paul's dead."

"Dead?" I could tell he couldn't believe it either. "How? When?"

"Today I reckon." I threw the cigarette into the yard. For a moment there was a silver spiral of smoke from the grass, then wind whipped it to nothingness. "Deputy said Sam Stevens shot him."

"How's Luke?"

"I don't know." I told about Luke's passing out and how the deputy was afraid to leave the old man by himself.

"I'd better clean up and go see if there's anything I can do." My father stood and looked off down the highway for a minute and then he said, "I guess this is what comes of drinking and carrying on like Paul did."

After he went in the house I sat watching cars turn off the highway onto Luke's white gravel lane. Word was getting out about Paul, and people were coming to see if they were needed, knowing there was nothing they could do, but coming anyway. The dust raised by one car didn't settle before another turned in, and I wondered how many of them were saying "This is what comes of drinking and carrying on."

I'd always heard talk that Paul was going to come to a bad end. I never believed it, and Paul didn't either. He had plans, and I was sorry those people had to be right about him.

21

When he had washed and changed clothes, my father came back outside. "You want to go up there?" he asked.

I shook my head.

"We'll be back directly." He walked to the gate and turned. "I didn't mean nothing bad about Paul," he said.

"I know," I told him.

Then he was gone and I watched the comings and goings of cars. So many people had known Paul was headed for something bad, but I never saw one of them try and stop it, or even try to understand why. It didn't seem fair, that they were right.

When my folks came back from Luke's they told me how Paul had died. Ernie Johnston had been with Sam Stevens and Paul, and he was spreading the story of the killing around town. The ones who heard him told other people till nearly everybody knew a version of the story they'd tell as though they'd been there and watched it happen.

Ernie and Paul were drinking at Sam's house in Midland all Friday night, and by noon Saturday they were almost out of whiskey. Sam wanted to use Paul's car to go get more. Hawkes County is dry, and the bootleg places are outside of town. Paul thought Sam was too drunk to drive, and told him to wait until he felt like going himself.

Being told to wait made Sam mad, and he cussed about it a long while, drinking what liquor they had left, getting madder and madder. Finally he took a pistol out of a drawer and said now he guessed Paul would give him the car keys. Paul just laughed, told him to go to hell.

And Sam started shooting him.

Ernie said after the first shot Paul fell down and begged Sam to stop, but the gun fired five times before Sam threw it behind the couch and ran out of the house. Ernie called an ambulance but Paul bled to death before it came. Sam was in jail even before Luke heard the news.

That was how Paul died.

My folks were at the mortuary most of that evening, but I stayed home. While they were gone I sat on the porch and looked at a single light shining in Luke's house.

At our place at the foot of the hill, on warm nights you could sit outside and Paul's music would drift down the lane, cross the highway to you, and it was fine to sit there and listen. By the time it traveled all that way it would be only a whisper of itself, just enough to know if Paul wanted company or needed to be left alone.

A lot of people in Hawkes County can play music, but Paul was the only one I ever knew who could make an instrument talk for him.

On a clear night the white gravel lane to Luke's house was a lazy river of milky light that looked like it had been poured from the moon. Paul would be sitting in an old cane-bottomed chair, soft-lit by a kerosene lantern that served as a porch light. Maybe he'd be playing his mandolin, holding it close like a woman holds a baby, and leaning against the house within reach would be the guitar and banjo.

If he wasn't finished with a piece of music as I walked out of the dark, Paul would nod hello and go on playing till the piece was done. Then he'd stop for a while, sipping from a pint bottle of bourbon. Sometimes I'd take a sip too, then chew Spearmint gum the rest of the night so my folks wouldn't smell whiskey when I went home.

Maybe Paul could lie when he talked. I've heard people say he sometimes would. But he never lied with music. Whatever was on his mind came from the strings as honest as anything can be. All he could do when his hands were on a guitar or banjo was show the truth about himself. Truth was loneliness, and some kind of hurt, inside Paul.

When he took a break from playing we'd talk, shadows moving around us as moths played near the lantern they didn't know would burn. When you're growing up there are things you need to talk about. Starting to smoke cigarettes is one of them, and going after a basketball game to get sick drunk with your friends on a secret case of warm beer is another.

Soft curves on girls who've always been awkward angles, and the way you burn to know more about the curves is another one of those things. Paul would listen and never laugh, and if he spoke at all, it was a right kind of thing to say. He was a good man to talk with.

I couldn't get hold of the notion Paul was really dead, so I had to go to the funeral. Walking into Brushy Creek Baptist Church, I felt it. The thing in the coffin was so still and quiet it had to be dead, and the thing in the coffin was Paul. So I knew, really *knew*. But for the feeling to be there so quick was a hurt, and before the service started I went outside.

I stood under a hot July sun, leaned against the hard warmth of someone's car while the choir sang *Precious Memories* and *I'll Fly Away*. I heard Reverend Stuckey preach about "In my Father's house are many mansions," and "I go to prepare a place for you." Then he talked about what he thought Paul was.

But he never mentioned guitars or mandolins, and he didn't say anything about brown pint bottles. He didn't say anything about being a good man to talk with.

He didn't talk about Paul at all.

FINDING THE GATE

A Sunday School choir was here today, ushered in by a slick faced grinning preacher so they could sing hymns for the old folks after dinner. As they were leaving, a boy looked at me and stuck an elbow in his friend's rib. "That one lady must be older than God," he said, his voice low enough he didn't think I heard.

The boys laughed, and so did I. They didn't mean to hurt my feelings. It was the sort of thing Stevie might have said. Besides, sometimes I *feel* older than God.

The young nurses who work in this place believe in options, in free choice. I hear them often, earnest and convinced, assuring one another every woman has opportunities beyond only doing what men want. Perhaps I had opportunities too, and settled on the wrong ones. But looking back, it seems to me things just happened.

Even with Stevie.

I'm old enough to have turned twenty just after the first big war, and by the standards of that day, I was educated. Nobody in my family ever finished high school, but I did, and spent two terms at the "Normal School," where the college is now. If anyone asked why I spent so much time at learning, I said I wanted to be a school teacher.

Once, at church, I heard a visiting preacher compare the high flint ridges rising all around us to the caring, cradling arms of Jesus. It was a pretty image, but to me these Kentucky mountains seemed more a fence so high we could neither cross nor see beyond it.

I talked about teaching school; what I *wanted* was a gate through that fence.

Then I met Steven Ray Bell, red-haired, broad-shouldered Steven Ray Bell from Ashland. Each evening for five months, he whistled *The Wildwood Flower* as he climbed the hill road to the boarding house where I stayed. Steven's intense daily march amazed me as I watched, standing away from the window so he couldn't see. No one ever courted me so earnestly.

I married Steven because he wanted me, because I was feeling a bit desperate with no other marriage prospects, because for a few months in 1922 I let fear convince me there *was* no gate.

We grew tobacco and paid our taxes. That's all Steven talked about: whether tobacco was doing well and might do better next year. That and high taxes. When his hunger to own more acres grew irresistible, Steven worked at the brickyard to make money to buy land, and I managed the fields without him. I chopped weeds and carried water for his precious tobacco, waiting for the day we'd be "settled," when I could teach and begin searching for the gate again.

By the time I was twenty-five I had four daughters, and felt old, emptied of everything but more babies. When I was twenty-six my son came, and he was my saving.

The birth was hard, and I spent a week in bed afterward. I hadn't done that when the others were born, and Steven was so frightened he brought me a present. He'd gone to Ott Taylor's auction, looking for tools, and carried home instead a bushel basket of old books. "You like to read," he said. "Maybe you can find something you like in here."

I threw dozens of the books out. An advanced Latin text didn't offer me anything, and most of the others were just as useless. But toward the bottom of the basket was the atlas, with maps and pictures of every place I'd heard of and ever so many I hadn't.

There were political divisions in a dozen colors, graphs of annual rainfall and principal products and population densities, racial distribution, heights above or below sea level, all a person could wish to know about any piece of earth important enough to have a name. I can close my eyes and still see the red and blue lines representing roads into all those far corners of the world. It was wonderful.

My baby had his father's hair color, and later the world would differentiate between "Big Steve" and "Little Steve," "Big Red" and "Little Red." So long as he lived, I never called my son anything but Stevie. He nearly killed me, screaming and kicking his way into life, impatient even from birth to be out and about this wide world. I lay in bed that first week, held him to my breast and studied the book.

Perhaps something happened while I lay nursing my baby, losing myself in maps, dreaming about a gate that never opened. Perhaps I gave Stevie more than milk, passed into him a yearning for his own gate. I believe he was already looking for it when he was six years old, the day he wandered away and stayed lost for hours.

At dusk his father came home from the tobacco patches. Exhausted by searching for Stevie, I was alone on the front porch, the girls fearfully quiet in the house. Our farm was divided by a creek, and I was ensnared in a vision of my son, caught somewhere in swirling muddy water.

Steven shouted at me, said I ought to have watched the boy more closely, demanded to know why the girls hadn't kept him from wandering. And he said other things, loud and hurtful. I *know* he was more frightened than angry, but some of what Steven said burns to this day.

Steven was lighting a lantern, preparing to go out and look for my son, when small movements parted the bushes around our house lot, and Stevie stepped into the clearing. Clothes, face, and hands streaked with dirt, he smiled at me. Not at his father, or at finding home again. He smiled at *me*.

Later, when his father's rage had passed, our daughters sent tearfully to bed, I took my son onto the porch and rocked him a long time in the summer darkness. By and by, Stevie began to tell me what he'd seen.

He found silver minnows in a dark creek, followed the water's flow to distant fields. Crouched in weeds, he saw his father's sweaty labor in mid-day heat, laughed at curses Steven flung at our mule. Fat groundhogs crept from hillside crevices, and their babies came out to play, ignoring Stevie as though he belonged in that wild place.

I rocked till my son slept, until he became a limp, warm weight in my arms. I thought of his small body hidden in high grass, watching strange business. I saw, as he had, mystery in a muddy creek. Stevie brought me what he had seen, and locked to a farm I'd grown to hate, I made him my saving.

I found my gate.

Stevie was lost for years after that, lost and wandering, seeing and doing. He came occasionally home, whiskey-breathed, sometimes with nameless women whose faces turned always to floors or far corners. Stevie's eyes were always bright with wonder and pleasure as theirs were haunted.

His father had no time or patience for the boy. Once Stevie brought a guitar and played it for me, singing a silly song he'd made up. One of his lyrics was "My mama gives me money but my daddy gives me hell. "

Until Stevie died, I bought a new atlas whenever the current one seemed dated, so he could show where he'd been since I'd seen him last. I never mentioned his whiskey; he never talked about the women.

But he told me how the desert bloomed an Eden; one Arizona summer he saw a rare August flood. He showed me marks a Dakota blizzard put on his feet the time he recklessly hopped a fast freight train from Pierre to Bismarck. He gave me Amarillo, San Francisco, Denver, Boston, Minnesota.

Bringing pieces of his restless wandering back to that damned farm, he was my gate and dear God, *he was my saving.*

THE PROCEDURE

The office is fifteen feet square, separate from the operations section of the lumber yard and mill where Tommy Sewell is half-owner. Tommy paid for the building's construction and furnishings out of his own pocket. Carl Fraley, his partner, agreed to the new building only because the mill required a larger finish planer, and the best place to install it was where Tommy's office used to be.

The office is heavily insulated. So long as the door's closed, the sound of trucks delivering raw logs or picking up finished lumber is only distant vibration. There's a window in each wall, and long before anyone arrives, Tommy knows they're coming. Dark plastic film covers each pane of glass. From the mill yard the windows are a black cipher, but Tommy can see out just fine.

So there's no surprise when Carl opens the door and admits the roar of machines and the shouted voices of their operators. Tommy's been watching Carl ever since he left the mill. "You still taking the Adkins girl to Lexington?" Carl asks when he's closed off the noise.

Tommy nods.

Carl—and Marcie Adkins—are the only people who know Tommy won't be alone when he goes out of town later. Tommy's wife thinks he's meeting a purchasing agent from a store chain that might buy thousands of two-by-fours next year. He'd told Cora Sue about a dinner with enough drinking he won't be in any shape to drive home, so it's an overnight trip.

Carl comes to stand by Tommy's desk, stares pointedly at a

29

framed photograph at the edge of the blotter. "You're risking a lot," he says, still looking at the fifteen-year-old Olan Mills pose.

The kids were sixteen, thirteen and ten when it was taken. Now the boys are raising their own families. Carla's twenty-five and a grad student at the University of Louisville. In the picture, Cora Sue's hair cascades below her shoulders, and she smiles the confidence of a woman men turn their heads to watch. Around the time Cora Sue and Tommy stopped making love and settled for going through the motions of sex every couple of weeks, she got her hair cut short.

"Cora Sue'll leave if she finds out what you've done," Carl says.

Tommy shrugs, looks past his partner to the window, watches a truck head out, loaded with hundreds of freshly milled boards. He knows Carl's right. With the kids gone, Tommy doesn't understand why Cora Sue's still with him. Taking a girl a year younger than his daughter to Lexington might be enough to wreck what's left of his marriage.

"I don't get it. You're acting crazy." Carl scowls, shakes his head. "You're fixing to throw your whole life away for a little bit of strange."

Tommy leans back into the embrace of his high-backed executive chair, puts his hands behind his head, and forces a smile. "Nothing's gonna happen, Carl," he says.

Carl turns to go, stops by the door to face the desk again. "Just don't do something stupid, tear up everything over a piece of young pussy."

Tommy's sure Carl isn't worried about the health of anyone's marriage. It's the lumber yard that concerns him, the impact of a divorce settlement on their partnership. Cora Sue would wind up owning a piece of the business, and her association with Carl would never be as functional as what the two men have built over two and a half decades.

Still smiling, Tommy says "Really, Carl, it'll be okay."

When his partner's gone and the noise from outside fades, Tommy reaches into his desk drawer, rummages through a pile of compact discs. He puts one in his computer's CD player, and as the sounds of Cajun accordion swell and fill from the speakers, stands to dance a passable two-step by himself, locking the office door as he spins by it.

Occasionally glancing out his windows, Tommy dances through three songs. For a man who's forty pounds overweight, he displays an unlikely grace. During a waltz he thinks about a long ago evening in a New Orleans bar.

A married lady danced with him all night, disappearing right before closing. There are several compact discs in the desk drawer to remind him of the lady and the night, but Tommy's never again danced with a partner to the sounds of a Cajun band.

At four o'clock he puts the CD away, turns off the computer, and leaves the office. His Explorer's just outside the door, baking in the sun since lunch. Tommy turns all the air conditioning vents toward the driver's seat before steering through the rutted, muddy yard. Near the gate he passes Carl, deep in conversation with one of their workers. Tommy lifts his hand in a wave, and when he reaches highway blacktop, shifts the SUV out of four wheel drive.

He drives the length of Midland, toward the interstate. The college town has grown since Tommy was a boy, but it still takes only a few minutes to get past all of downtown. A mile and a half east of the I-64 turn-off he stops at the bookstore where Cora Sue's worked since their daughter graduated high school.

He finds his wife stocking shelves. On Thursdays, U.P.S. delivers cases of new books from the store's distributor, and it's Cora Sue's busiest shift of the week. She glances briefly at Tommy when he comes to stand close to her, then turns back to an open box of Steven King's latest. "You leaving?" she asks.

Tommy nods, though Cora doesn't look at him again, can't see the gesture. "I'm meeting that buyer at eight. I want to get checked into a room first."

His wife turns from the shelves to plant a dry kiss on his cheek. "Have a nice time."

"Sure you don't want to go?" Tommy puts his hands on Cora Sue's waist.

She shakes her head, as he knew she would. "Lumber and shipping schedules are boring." Facing the shelves again, she moves forward just enough to step away from his hands.

Tommy watches her for a piece of time, though he's been dismissed. He thinks about offering to buy the bookstore again. They could afford it, and the store's a money-maker. But the last time he mentioned such a plan, Cora Sue looked at him with wide eyes and asked, "Why would I want to do that?"

Her response surprised Tommy. Cora Sue forever complains about Ralph Conley's poor management. Tommy was sure his wife would welcome a chance to show her boss the door, change things to suit her own notions of how books and greeting cards should be sold.

Leaving the store he wonders if, for Cora Sue, the bookstore is the equivalent of his office at the mill, a safe, comfortable place for passing time when there's no place else to be. Maybe she waltzes carts piled with books like he dances solo in his office.

Outside, he has to wait for a delivery truck to move, and fools with the Explorer's air conditioning again before heading out of town. Near the interstate ramp he turns into the parking lot of a Lee's Fried Chicken. Even before he sets the brake, Marcie runs out the restaurant door to climb in beside him.

Fastening her seat belt, the much younger woman smiles at him briefly, then sighs. "Tracey Whitman wanted to stay and see who I was sneaking off with. I thought I'd never get her to leave."

Tommy glances around the parking lot, wondering what kind of car Marcie's friend drives.

"She's not here," Marcie reassures him. "I called her at home about ten minutes ago and spoke to her, just to make sure."

Marcie twists in the seat to face her boss, arms folded across her chest. "Why's it so *cold* in here?"

Nipples swell against Marcie's blouse, visible even through her brassiere. Tommy thinks he ought to feel guilty for looking. The fact he doesn't seems worse than the looking itself. "You sure you want to go through with this?" he asks, though at the parking lot exit he doesn't hesitate before steering toward I-64.

"Surer than I'll ever be about anything." Marcie's voice is hardly more than a whisper.

The clean, subtle scent of her perfume reaches across the Explorer, and Tommy takes a deep breath, holds it a few seconds. There's a trace of Marcie in his lungs now, molecules that were recently on her skin. He feels himself blush, his face hot despite the air conditioner.

Marcie's worked at the lumber yard since she graduated from high school, but Tommy's known her much longer. When she was seven or eight years old he owned a trailer park at the edge of Midland, where her parents were tenants. Marcie's father was a truck driver, and Tommy can vaguely recall a skinny little girl standing near the coffin, after the accident. Her mother worked in the mill offices for a time, and he remembers Lou saying something about a daughter going to live with a grandmother in an adjacent county.

The day Marcie came asking for a job, years after her mother left for better pay at the jeans factory, Tommy was halfway through the interview before realizing the young woman nervously answering his questions was Lou's skinny daughter. The week they worked late hours together, getting the mill's tax papers ready for the accountant, Tommy fell in love with Marcie.

Fell in something anyway.

Marcie Adkins was bright, quickly grasping how the tax forms had to be organized, what mattered and what didn't. And she was a talker, telling him all about herself.

She lived with her grandmother, a life-long Pentecostal whose house was just across the Hawkes County line, a woman who disapproved of Marcie's working. The old woman didn't understand why the girl didn't marry one of several interested young men who called every night to ask her out. And Granny didn't see a reason for Marcie to go to college, even if they'd been able to afford it.

With a fifty-cent-an-hour raise, Tommy made Marcie his "assistant," which only meant she carried stacks of paper between the mill and his office. She carried papers and they talked, spending more and more time together. Tommy considered moving a desk for her into his retreat, but Marcie's eyes flinched the day he mentioned it.

That year was a boom time in the lumber business, and it wasn't hard to talk Carl into reimbursing employees for college courses, even giving them time off to attend classes. A few signed up for computer workshops at the college on the hill behind town. Marcie finished a degree in accounting.

Tommy's proud of his "assistant," proud of what he's done for her. He was the one who told her she was smart and attractive, who reminded her she needed to see the world beyond Midland, Kentucky, the one who made college possible. He glories in her change, from a bashful girl who giggled when someone older addressed her directly, into a confident young woman.

He's sure Marcie doesn't know she so often fills his mind. Rare times he touches his wife's doughy flesh, Tommy pretends his hands are on the younger woman's taut body. He adores Marcie, and if in some of his fantasies she reciprocates, in real life he does nothing, says nothing that would expose his feelings.

When she got pregnant, Tommy lent Marcie five hundred dollars, and let her use his office phone to make an appointment at a Lexington women's clinic. After the call he suggested she might not want to drive herself, that staying overnight before "the procedure" was a good idea. He was surprised she agreed.

Marcie reports plenty of details about her personal life, but never allows Tommy to be part of anything that happens away from the mill. He knows things about her friend Tracey, and about Jimmy, the baby's father, but wouldn't recognize either of them on the street.

"You care if I play some music?" Marcie asks after ten silent interstate miles.

Tommy shrugs, but shivers inwardly at the sounds from the car's speakers, hip-hop, rap, house music, whatever it is. He can't tell the difference. Marcie's music grates on Tommy's soul and in ten minutes he reaches for the volume control.

"We're staying at the Ramada," he says. "They've got room service there, so we won't have to go out for anything." When Marcie doesn't speak, he adds, "We *could* go out if you wanted to."

"Doesn't matter." She points at a sign indicating a rest area. "Could you stop, let me change clothes?"

While Marcie goes inside the brick building in the middle of the rest area Tommy shuts the radio off. There are CDs in the glove box, folky stuff and old time string bands, but that kind of music bothers Marcie as much as her rap music disturbs Tommy.

When Marcie comes back she's transformed. Tommy's grown used to the way the girl placates her over-Jesused grandmother. Each morning Marcie leaves the old woman's house wearing ankle-length dresses and the pinned hair of a Pentecostal maiden. She carries a change of clothes in a huge purse, and remakes herself at work. Evenings she reverses the process.

When he picked her up, she'd worn a long dark skirt with a sleeved white blouse, black hair rounded high on her head. At the rest area Marcie's put on a much shorter bright blue dress that leaves her arms bare, and loose hair hangs almost to her waist. Other young woman at the mill laugh at Marcie's costume changes, but Tommy finds the transformations endearing.

He stops once at a fast food restaurant for a cup of coffee to go, and they talk about out-of-town job offers that'll be forthcoming, now that Marcie has her degree. When she turns the radio on again, she finds a public radio station's violins, recites facts about the composer from a music appreciation class. Tommy smiles as he listens, contrasting the Marcie talking about a long-dead German musician with the bashful child who walked into his office to ask for a job.

There's a problem at the Ramada. The hotel has over-booked, and the only room available is a single with two double beds, rather than the connecting rooms Tommy requested. A convention in town will make finding other accommodations difficult, if not impossible. "It's okay," he tells Marcie when he comes out to the car. "We'll find something else even if we have to go all the way to Winchester."

"Let's stay," she counters. "I'm tired of riding." She looks past him, making up her mind about something. "Besides, I'd just as soon not be by myself tonight."

Tommy checks them in, finds a parking place and carries the bags inside. Once in the room he can't be still, bustles around turning on lamps, adjusting the ventilation, unpacking and hanging his clothes from the recessed rack by the door. When there's nothing else to do, the beds in the center of the room loom big as barges.

Bashful as a high school boy, Tommy retreats to the toilet, opens his fly and feels a hot blush in his face as he realizes the noise will be heard beyond the door. Coming back into the room he can't look at Marcie.

"Which bed do you want?" she asks, and when Tommy tells her it doesn't matter, she pulls the spread down on the one nearest the door. "I'm going to take a nap."

Tommy nods. "Want me to go someplace while you sleep? I could go to the lounge."

Marcie's brown eyes seem to be asking for something. Tommy would trade the world to know what it is because he'd give her anything, everything. She lies down, modestly pulls the spread over her legs. "Maybe you could stay? Watch TV or something?"

Tommy fiddles with the remote control until he finds CNN, then tours the room, turning off lights he's just turned on.

A talking head on the television makes noises about stock market scandals, and Tommy adjusts the volume until the electronic voice is hardly a whisper, no louder than Marcie's faint snore. He closes his eyes and feels something he can't put a name to, an emotional fumbling that brings tears to his eyes. He fights to keep his breathing from giving his feelings away.

Tommy feels foolish, clumsy and awkward, entirely aware his life is a total waste, a vast emptiness. He can't imagine suicide, but wishes some quick, painless disease would come for him. After a time he turns his thoughts toward the white beach fantasy.

He pictures tropical sand white as rock salt, gritty and hot against his skin. A small blue sailboat is anchored just off the beach, under a searing sun unlike any that ever hung over Hawkes County Kentucky. Marcie's stretched out beside him, a tiny bathing suit emphasizing long legs, perfect skin and flowing black hair. As Tommy drifts into a light doze, dream-Marcie's hand finds his own, entwines her fingers in his, and for dream-Tommy everything is fine with the world.

He wakes to Marcie's hand on his shoulder, shaking him. "Are you all right?" She sounds frightened. "You were making noises in your sleep, like you were crying."

As Tommy sits up in the bed Marcie takes a backward step. The bathroom light is on, and he can see his watch. It's almost nine o'clock, he's hungry and sleep-stupid. "It's okay," he says. "Just a dream."

Marcie sits on the other bed. "I decided I'd like to go out, if that's okay," she tells him. "Someplace where I won't think about tomorrow morning."

"Okay." Tommy goes to the bathroom, leaves the door open while he splashes water in his face.

"I'm not really hungry though." Marcie comes to stand in the doorway. "I ate in Midland, remember? Pick someplace you like."

Tommy towels water off his face and wishes he had the nerve to squeeze past Marcie. The doorway's narrow enough their bodies would touch.

He hates wearing suits, but Tommy's brought one. Otherwise Cora Sue might have been suspicious. He resigns himself to a necktie and coat for the evening. "A dress-up place?"

Marcie nods. "Real fancy, maybe."

It's awkward, changing clothes in the bathroom, and when it's Marcie's turn to dress, Tommy says he'll meet her in the lounge by the lobby. He has two double bloody marys while he waits, and when he mentions dinner, the bartender suggests an expensive seafood restaurant not far away. Tommy's back is to the door, but the bartender's appreciative leer tells him when Marcie comes into the lounge.

Turning to look, Tommy feels his own eyes grow wide. Marcie's put on a simple strapless black gown, the sort of dress he never expected to see her wear. Her hair's become a complicated braid, she wears tiny diamond earrings, and a small gold cross is suspended from a delicate chain at her neck.

Marcie crosses the room confidently, but when Tommy continues to stare she flushes from her shoulders to her eyebrows. "What?" she asks, like a child afraid she's done something wrong.

"Nothing," he tells her. "It's just that you're so beautiful."

Marcie flushes a darker shade. "It's only a used dress," she says. "I found it in a thrift shop when I went to Dayton last year with my aunt."

Tommy breaks off his staring and notices others in the lounge looking in their direction. Some of the men glance away from the young woman to study him appraisingly. Basking in their envy is a sweet sort of sin.

"Can I have a drink?" Marcie asks.

"What would you like?" Tommy says. "Champagne?"

She shakes her head. "I had that once. I want something new." She nods toward his glass. "What're you drinking?"

"A bloody mary."

When Tommy extends his glass Marcie sips delicately through the straw, wrinkling her nose. "Tastes like tomato juice with pepper," she says. "What else do they have?"

Tommy waves to the bartender. "'Nother of these for me," he tells the man. "And could you bring a . . ." He thinks a moment. "She'll have a white Russian," he decides, and leads Marcie to a table.

When they're settled in and their order is delivered, Marcie tastes her drink and laughs. "You're fooling me, right?"

"What do you mean?" Tommy's very happy. The percolation of alcohol through his bloodstream is a wonderful sensation.

"I wanted a drink, and this is like, I don't know, chocolate milk."

"Vodka, Kaluha, and cream," he tells her, then has to explain what Kaluha is. "Those things are a whole lot stouter than they taste. You need to be careful with them."

"No kidding?" Marcie raises her glass and drains it. "Is that being careful?" she asks, and laughs.

It's the first time she's laughed since they left Midland. Tommy laughs too, and orders more drinks. They go down fast, and he decides he doesn't trust himself to drive them to the restaurant. When he comes back to the table after asking the bartender to call a taxi, he says. "I *told* Cora Sue I'd get too drunk to drive."

"Did I get you drunk?" Marcie teases, and laughs again. "What did your wife say?" She poses this second question in a sober, serious tone.

Tommy raises his eyebrows, sighs. "Not much."

"You must have a really good marriage," Marcie says, stirring her drink with a plastic straw.

"Why do you say that?" Tommy couldn't have been more surprised if Marcie had told him she could fly.

"You're able to be honest with her. She let you bring me over here."

Tommy wants to lie, or at least leave the misunderstanding alone, but the alcohol won't let him be quiet. "Cora Sue doesn't know you're with me."

"She doesn't?"

He shakes his head.

Marcie doesn't say anything else until the bartender tells them the cab's waiting, just sits playing with the straw and her third drink. Before they go she hurriedly finishes it.

She's slightly over-dressed for the restaurant, and Tommy's aware of stares from other tables. The men look at him jealously, but the sidelong glances of the women are hostile. Sweet sin, he tells himself.

Dinner turns into a somewhat giddy few minutes when Tommy orders more drinks, convincing Marcie a bloody mary might go better with seafood than another white russian. "That or white wine, maybe beer," he adds.

"Can't stand the taste of beer," she tells him, leaning over the table as though telling him a secret. "Jimmy drinks a lot of it but when I tried it once I threw up." As Marcie giggles Tommy notices her eyes are a bit glazed.

He orders shrimp, though he doesn't eat much, and convinces Marcie to try a raw oyster. To his surprise she likes them, and orders six of her own. Tommy hasn't had so much fun at a meal in years, and he's sorry when the waiter brings the check, pointedly looking toward the entrance where there's a long line.

He gives the waiter a credit card, and while waiting for the signature form to be brought back, Tommy tells Marcie that in New Orleans they could get a couple of drinks to go. "Just ask for a 'go cup' is all we'd have to do," he says, and feels like a world traveler. Or at least a man who's been someplace other than Hawkes County.

Tommy wonders what Marcie would say if she knew he'd never spent so much as an entire week of his life outside Midland, Kentucky. He's over fifty, and has never been away from home so long as a week.

When the taxi comes Tommy puts his hand on Marcie as he guides her toward the vehicle. The connection from the small of her back to his palm burns hot as the sun on his fantasy beach. He wishes she'd stumble, catch her heel in the sidewalk and pitch backward so he could catch her in his arms. He wishes she'd stumble, but if she did Tommy knows he'd say things he can't imagine Marcie wants to hear.

Once the taxi's moving, Tommy's good mood evaporates, and he leans into the seat, letting his head fall backward, the quick, painless disease fantasy flickering again. Something fast, something to save him from feeling so often old, so often foolish, so often alone.

He's dozing, almost ready to invoke the beach and the blue sailboat when a happy squeak from Marcie brings him awake. "I wanna stop there," she says. "Really. I wanna go in and see that place. Please?"

Tommy raises his head, sees Marcie's already ordered the cab to pull over. Not quite awake, he gives the driver a twenty and waves off his change. The taxi pulls away, and he acquiesces to Marcie's tug on his arm.

"Can we go in?" she asks. "Just for a little while? I wanna see what they do in there."

Tommy looks around, sees they're on New Circle Road someplace. Still sleep-fogged, he looks up at the words "LIVE NUDE GIRLS" outlined in neon overhead, then looks quickly away, tries to find what Marcie wanted to stop for even as she pulls him through the strip joint's door.

"Jimmy and his buddies come to these places all the time." Marcie has to shout above the blaring music. Her eyes are bright and happy and she's grinning. "He thinks I don't know but I do. I want to see what they do here."

Tommy lets himself be pulled deeper into the darkness beyond the bar's entrance, and as the door swings shut he makes Marcie stop so his eyes can adjust. The place is all black light and mirrors over three small stages, naked women on each of them. On the center stage a platinum blonde hangs off a brass pole that belongs in a firehouse, hangs from it backward, and she's utterly naked.

Marcie's pulling at him again, until they're at a table and she's shouting drink orders at a woman whose breasts are exposed. Tommy blushes but Marcie only laughs and puts her mouth close to his ear to shout "I always wanted to come in one of these places but never *ever* thought I'd get to."

Tommy thinks he ought to say something, but can't, and contents himself with watching Marcie finish her drink while he's still paying for it. Looking at Marcie is easier than looking at their waitress, or the naked women on the stages. When he hollers a question Marcie nods and he orders another drink.

Later, when Tommy thinks about the time he and Marcie spent inside the bar, he can't recall what happened in any sort of linear fashion. His memory is a series of disconnected images, and he has no idea which came first, last or in the middle.

He remembers switching to bourbon and Coke when the bloody mary he ordered tasted rancid and looked awful. Every time he orders a drink for himself, Marcie's ready too, and asks the waitress for "something different" each time. Her drinks come in different colors, some in two or three layers of color. Marcie swallows them quickly, and he remembers her saying over and over she didn't know liquor could taste like candy.

There's a time when a dancer's sitting next to Marcie, the women's heads close together in a female conspiracy, and Marcie asks for twenty dollars. As one of the naked women straddles his knees he realizes Marcie's bought him one of the "lap dances" advertised by a flashing marquee over the bar.

The young woman gyrates on his legs the length of one song from too loud speakers. The experience is supposed to be erotic, but even when the dancer leans so far forward her breasts graze Tommy's face, he thinks only about how foolish he must appear. When he looks at Marcie she's laughing and mouths something he can't hear, something he thinks is meant to encourage him. He has no idea what she wants him to do though.

He remembers stumbling to the men's room, which is surprisingly clean, and empty. Standing over the urinal he thinks for a while he might get sick, wonders if the bar will evict him if he throws up, but the feeling passes. Zipping his trousers Tommy leans forward until his forehead is against the cool tile of the wall, wishes he was anyplace but where he is.

Later he somehow came to be standing at the bar, going through the motions of conversation with a man his own age without ever hearing one word of what was said.

He's aware of being helped into a cab, but the ride is a blank, and then he's leaning on Marcie as she guides him to their room.

When he wakes in the near-total darkness of the room, mouth dry, head ringing with hangover percussion, it takes a while to remember he's at the Ramada. The curtain is drawn, slivers of bright sunshine spiking into the room, making his head ache. The bed next to him is empty, and the bathroom door is ajar. He's alone.

He lurches out of bed, stands unsteadily over the toilet as his bladder empties, and doesn't see the note taped to the mirror until he's flushed and turned toward the door.

"I called Jimmy, and he's going to the clinic with me," Tommy reads. "I don't think I'm coming back to work at the mill. Jimmy wants me to move to Lexington. I'll call you tomorrow." There are circles over each *i* in the note, and Marcie's drawn a heart around her signature.

Tommy stumbles to the bed, lies in darkness with one arm over his eyes, and believes he might cry. He thinks about a beach with white sand, a blue sailboat, and fast acting diseases.

THE WHOLE STORY, 1969

"You going a-fishing?" Pete Rafferty asked when I walked up to his grocery. He was sitting on a rusty lawn chair, taking advantage of what little shade there was around his place.

I gave him a quarter and got myself an RC Cola from the cooler inside. "Too hot for fishing," I said.

Rudy Duckworth was perched on a tilted Dr. Pepper crate, Tom Ferguson hunkered down next to him. I could smell the whiskey they'd been drinking. A year or two later Pete got religion and wouldn't allow alcohol anywhere around him, but back then he took a drink any time one was offered.

Rudy and Tom had stopped by Pete's after going to Langley Carson's. Hawkes County was dry, and Langley was our bootlegger. He had a place across from Pete's grocery on top of the hill, where he sold beer and whiskey, with some cheap wine for old timers whose sense of taste had been completely destroyed by years of drinking.

The union had shut down every coal operation in the county, which was why all of us had time to sit around with Pete. Just a couple months out of high school, I was waiting for the draft board to remember my name. The only work I could find was stacking two-by-fours at the lumber yard three or four days a week, but everything in Hawkes County depended on the mines. Three weeks into the strike I was laid off.

I squatted in the shade, hoping Tom and Rudy would send me to Langley's for more liquor. If I went and got it they'd feel like they had to offer me a drink.

Directly Pete looked off down the road, shading his eyes with his hand. "Ain't that Dick Allen's mother a-walking this way?"

"Sho' is," Rudy agreed.

"Dick wasn't at Langley's, was he?" Pete asked.

Rudy shook his head. "I don't remember seeing him there."

Dick Allen had been in the Korean War and came home missing a leg. He worked odd jobs when he could get them, but what he mostly did was drink. Just about every day he'd buy a bottle and sit at Langley's till it was gone. Then he'd get another to last him through the evening, and limp home on the artificial leg the government gave him.

"Dick was a smart boy till the whiskey got him," Pete told us.

"Shame that old woman's out in this heat," said Rudy. "What could you have in this little old store she'd walk all this way to get?"

"She ain't coming here. They's three stores closer to her house than this." Pete leaned out from his chair and spit into the dust. "Could be fetching Dick a jug. Man like that can shake to pieces if he needs a drink and ain't got one."

Rudy shook his head and grinned. "I know Bertha Allen. That old lady'd sooner touch a snake than a whiskey bottle."

We watched her come, red faced after walking the better part of three miles. Pete called out, "Awful warm for walking, Mrs. Allen," and stood up. "Come in the shade and cool off."

She took a few more steps, then stopped. "Any of you all seen my boy?" she asked. "Has he been up to that Carson place today?"

"Ain't seen him a'tall, Mrs. Allen," Rudy told her.

She looked us in the eye, one at a time. "Let me ask you a question." Mrs. Allen eased a pace or two closer. "Do you think Langley Carson will listen if I ask him not to sell my Dickie any more whiskey?"

I couldn't help snickering, and Pete told me to hush. Her son stood six four and was hard as concrete, even if he *was* a one legged drunk. He'd a beat the socks off anyone else in the county that called him "Dickie."

"Come set down, Mrs. Allen," Pete said again.

"Just answer my question."

"You ain't got no business around a place like Langley's, Mrs. Allen," Pete argued. "One of us can talk to him for you."

"I want to know if you think that no good Carson will listen if I ask him." The old woman didn't move. When none of us said anything she looked straight at *me*. "Seems like you'd have something better to do than hang around these no-accounts. I can smell that liquor stink all the way across the road." And she set off walking again, not looking back.

"Let me drive you up," Tom Ferguson called.

"No." Bertha Allen stopped in the middle of the road and lifted her hands. Closing her eyes, she raised her voice, like she wanted them to hear all the way to White Dove Pentecostal Church. "My Jesus will help me up that hill. And He'll get me there without making me ride with a drunkard."

It took Mrs. Allen half an hour to climb to Langley's, but she didn't stay five minutes. Coming down, she sang a hymn in that off-key way the Pentecostals have. At the foot of the hill she glared at us, but didn't stop, and didn't speak.

When she'd gone, Rudy told me, "Go get us a couple pints of Old Grand Dad, Billy. Ask Langley what she said." He handed me four one dollar bills, and as I stood up he added, "Don't break the seal on them bottles till you get back."

"Take my car." Tom tossed me his keys, interested as me or Rudy to find out what happened between Langley and Mrs. Allen.

"Don't open that whiskey," Rudy said again as I got into Tom's banged-up Ford.

It didn't take any time at all to drive up the lane that had been a trial for Bertha Allen. Once the hilltop had been a farm with a house and barn, but Langley sold the barn for scrap lumber. He peddled booze out of the house till it burned one night, and after that the brick cellar, all that was left of the farm, was his liquor store.

I didn't have to get out of the car. Langley'd bring the whiskey to me, but I wanted to talk to him. "Got any Old Grand Dad?" I called as I walked across gravel to the cellar.

"Who's it for?" Langley wanted to know.

He was telling me I was too young to buy whiskey for myself, and I wished I'd made him walk out into the heat to the car. "Tom Ferguson wants it. And Rudy Duckworth, down at Pete's."

The bootlegger was inside the dark cellar, out of the sun, and I couldn't see him clearly till I stood in the doorway. Langley Carson was almost seventy, but he wasn't someone to trifle with. There was a holstered gun at his waist, a reminder that men had tried to rob him two or three times. "Pint?" he asked, reaching toward the rows of bottles.

I put Rudy's money on a beat up old end table. "Two."

"Dick Allen's mama talk to you all before she come up here?" Langley slipped the bottles into paper bags.

"She stopped for a minute."

"Her boy may be 'little Dickie' to her, but he'll be trouble for me before this is over." Langley shook his head and settled into a shaky wooden chair by the end table. "If she didn't want me to sell him whiskey she should a come to see me when he was a young pup, 'stead of waiting till now."

"What you gonna do?"

"I don't know." Langley looked toward a two-year-old calendar hanging on the wall, like there was something there for him to puzzle out. When he didn't say anything else I turned to go, and I was almost to the car when he came outside. "I don't need anybody else up here. Tell 'em that," he called. "And tell 'em to stop Dick Allen from coming." The bootlegger breathed a loud sigh. "If they can."

All my life I'd heard tales about when this or that happened in Hawkes County. The business between Langley and Mrs. Allen sounded like it could turn into a good story, and watching it close up seemed like a fine place to be. I kicked gravel, driving onto the lane leading off the hill, in a hurry to get back to Pete's with my piece of story.

After I gave the bottles and thirty cents change to Rudy, he offered me first drink from the first bottle. I took it, even though my folks would have whipped me if they'd seen me swallowing whiskey, big as I was.

"What'd Langley say?" Tom asked after all of us had the bottle once.

"To keep Dick Allen off that hill if you can." I told them.

"Maybe one of us should go up there," Rudy said.

"Langley said not to." I gave the bottle to Pete. "He just wants you to keep Dick away."

When the bottle came back to me, I took a big jolt. I figured this was the last time they'd offer it, and I fought down a long swallow. "Why does that old woman make any difference to a bootlegger anyway?" I asked.

"Langley had a mother just like the rest of us. He feels sorry for Bertha Allen." Rudy cut a piece of tobacco off the plug he carried and stuffed it into his cheek. "Besides, if church people hear Langley sold whiskey to Dick Allen after his poor old mama begged him not to, they'll pressure the sheriff to close Langley down. Pentecostals never miss a vote."

"Sheriff knows they don't, too," Pete added.

Rudy nodded. "Langley's got a problem."

I stayed there with them a long while, and didn't even care that the whiskey wasn't offered to me again. It felt like a show was about to be put on for anyone lucky enough to be sitting at Pete's, and I was glad to be in a position to see it. Dick Allen never came around, though I stayed at the store till almost five o'clock. Before going home I chewed a whole package of spearmint gum to hide what was left of the liquor smell.

After supper my father settled down with the Louisville paper while Mama cleaned up the kitchen. I couldn't stop thinking about what would happen at Langley's, or wishing I was at Pete's. It would be interesting once Dick Allen got there.

"I believe I'll go out for a while," I said when I couldn't pretend anymore to be interested in the television.

"Where to?" Daddy asked.

"See if Joe Taylor wants to shoot baskets at the high school." I was surprised at the easy lie, resented the need for it.

"Be in early," Daddy told me.

I left without answering. I didn't like to be talked to like I still needed permission to come and go.

I headed straight to Pete's, in such a hurry I almost ran the last hundred yards. Tom and Rudy were still there, congregated with a few others outside the grocery, all of them staring up the hill to Langley's. Tom Ferguson glanced at me. "Dick come by about ten minutes ago, drunk as I ever seen him."

"What'd he say?" someone asked, like they'd just got there too.

"Dick's plenty mad," Rudy answered. "His mama went home and when she found him drunk, she told him Langley wouldn't sell him whiskey ever again. Dick told her he'd buy whiskey if he wanted to." Not a man standing at Pete's hadn't heard tales about how wild Dick'd get if something set him off when he was drinking.

"He climbed that hill awful fast for a one legged feller," Tom said, and some of us laughed.

I told what happened when I was at the bootlegger's earlier in the day. "I don't think Langley'll take any foolishness off of him," I said after my part was finished, pleased when some of the other men agreed with me, and said so.

"Dick had a pistol," Pete told us. "In the waist of his pants, under his shirt."

Just as Pete quit talking, we heard the shot.

"Holy Jesus," somebody muttered.

"Whose pistol was it?" someone else asked. "Dick's? Or Langley's?"

"No telling," Pete said. "Billy, go call the law."

"What?"

Pete explained what he wanted me to do, slowly, as if he were talking to an idiot. "Go in the store and call the sheriff. Tell him Dick or Langley one is shot."

"Somebody's bound to be dead," Rudy muttered.

By the time I got back outside, Langley had driven his pickup down to Pete's, and nobody was dead, nor even shot. Dick Allen lay in the back of Langley's truck, moaning and thrashing around, his face split like an overripe plum. Langley'd parked at the other end of the store from us, but no one moved closer to him.

A siren coming from town was echoing off the hills before Langley spoke. He slumped against his truck and crossed his arms. "Son of a bitch shot off a pistol," he said. "Had to hit him in the head with a brick." Langley leaned to the side like he wanted to spit, but nothing came out of his mouth.

The sheriff got to Pete's in no time at all, and Mrs. Allen was climbing out of the county car even before it stopped rolling. "What've you all done to my boy?" she shrieked, red lights flashing in her eyes, making her look even crazier than usual. "Has somebody killed my Dickie?"

Langley ignored her and said a few words to the deputy, who cuffed Dick's hands behind his back. Before they got him in the sheriff's car Dick turned and saw his mother standing there.

"God damn you Mama," he said. "God *damn* you. You've got me put in jail." He raised his good leg to kick at her, but the deputy jerked hard on the handcuffs and Dick fell over.

"God *damn* you," he said again, sobbing as the deputy picked him up and shoved him toward the car.

Mrs. Allen dropped down onto her knees, crying and praying at the same time. Langley looked at her and said, "Somebody tell that old woman I never sold her Dickie no more whiskey. Tell her I done just what she wanted."

Langley walked to his truck. "Damn near got me shot," he muttered. "But by God I never sold him nothing."

Langley sounded like he was about to cry too.

I watched the sheriff trying to close a car door behind Dick, and then looked at his mother. I'd never seen anything as pitiful as that old lady, on her knees in the dirt, crying.

How that old woman looked wouldn't be part of the story people told, about the time Dick Allen's mama made Langley stop selling him whiskey.

I wished I'd stayed home and watched television.

FIRE, AND STELLA

Randall Sparks intended to end his October Saturday night with a triple bourbon and water. Alone except for a half-tame tomcat claiming one end of the porch swing, Randall sipped his drink and assumed the faint smoke-haze in the air came from a head-high pile of poplar and red maple trees, dragged off the hills around Joe Caudill's farm.

Friday, Joe had stopped by Randall's after work, said if good weather held for the weekend, he'd burn the brush where it lay. It wasn't fit for winter firewood, not when the forested hills were littered with hardwood brought down by wind. Poplar and red maple were trash trees, starving more valuable seedlings of sunlight.

"Call me if you need a hand," Randall offered, leaning against his mailbox. As dust from his neighbor's pickup settled, Randall had felt wretchedly stupid, saying such a thing to a one-armed man.

Joe Caudill never accepted assistance from neighbors. He'd cut the useless trees alone, controlling a chainsaw with one arm and a stump where an elbow used to be. His saw was only a fourteen-incher, but even mini-Homelites buck if the bar's pinched, just like the big ones. Joe's little saw could cut through a man's leg fast as a Stihl or McCullough.

Once in a while Randall wished Joe *would* call for help. How his neighbor accomplished some tasks with one arm seemed mysterious and worth learning. Cutting wood with a chainsaw was one such chore. Mounting implements on a tractor's three-point hitch was another.

And there was the business with Stella Oakley. One arm would be a factor in that, too.

Wood smoke was a fine complement to the taste of iced Saturday bourbon, and Randall's eyes grew heavy with sleep. Inhaling deeply, he allowed his mind to wander away from Joe Caudill. He was near deciding it was time to stumble to bed when he heard fire trucks on the highway.

Randall didn't connect sirens with his neighbor until the shrieking vehicles turned onto the narrow lane that ended at the Caudill place. When the second truck passed the porch he hurried inside and told Mildred there was a fire at Joe's.

"Is it the house?" she fretted, sitting straighter in her chair, turning from the eleven o'clock news. "Are Delia and Joe all right?"

"I don't know." Randall grabbed a baseball cap from the hook by the back door and felt his shirt pocket for cigarettes. "I can't see that far from the porch."

By the time he reached the Caudill house Joe's barn was a fireball, weathered planks and beams outlined in orange flame. Hay bales stacked rafter high ensured the loss of everything below the tin roof. Randall stared in awe, breathless and sweating. Pumps and engines on the fire trucks made an awesome din, but the sighing hungry breath of fire lay over those mechanical noises.

Glancing to his left, Randall watched a trio of firemen direct a spray of water onto the roof of Joe's house. They'd already given up the barn, and there was nothing left for them to do but ensure drifting hot ash didn't take the house as well.

Flood lamps mounted on the fire trucks pointed in all directions. No matter how he turned his head, another few hundred watts glared full in Randall's face. It took a while to locate Joe, leaning on a thick twisted oak, two panting beagles sprawled at his feet. Randall looked back to the barn, where the kennel used to be.

"They climbed the fence." A small grin twitched the corners of Joe's mouth. "Got over it before I had any idea what was happening."

Randall stared at the fire a long time without saying anything. Joe's wasn't the first barn burning he'd seen, but it was the fastest. The fire spent itself in less than an hour, roar became whisper, and the night filled with the steady throb of pumps and engines.

"It's Merle again," Randall said in the relative quiet. He didn't look at Joe Caudill directly, but eased his glance far enough to peripherally see his neighbor's noncommittal shrug. "You call the sheriff?" The negative shake of Joe's head was small, but definite.

Later Randall sat at the kitchen table with Joe and Delia, sipping coffee, listening as they speculated about the timing and quantity of an insurance settlement. He silently wondered how much the woman knew about trouble between her husband and Merle Oakley. Randall was uncomfortable in the kitchen, afraid he'd say the wrong thing if he stayed too long.

He used the Caudill's telephone to tell Mildred no one was dead and the house wasn't burned. Delia refilled his cup, but Randall drank the rest of his coffee outside, under the big oak.

Firemen were rolling what seemed like miles of hose onto their trucks. With the loud pumps turned off it was easier to talk. "Be awful damn foolish not to call Jesse Surratt," Randall told Joe. "Merle's gone past pranks."

"This ain't the sheriff's business." Joe didn't say anything more, just shook his head, staring at the ruin of his barn.

Randall wanted to shout *"Was screwing Stella Oakley half a dozen times worth roofing nails in your driveway, sugar in your tractor's gas tank, and a burnt barn?"* That was as much as he personally knew about, though he suspected it was less than a full accounting of what Merle Oakley had done.

He didn't ask about Stella though. Instead, he looked at the ground, head throbbing from breathing raw wood smoke on top of a building hangover. He wondered if Joe was afraid of Merle Oakley. Randall knew *he* would have been afraid. Merle wasn't a man to back away from trouble.

His usual trouble was fights at saloons in town, and he didn't mind fighting men bigger than himself. Merle Oakley would be more than a match for the one-armed man who went six times to the

Trail View Motel with Stella, while Merle was thirty days in jail for his third D.U.I.

After a while Randall asked, "What *are* you going to do?"

Joe only shrugged and exhaled a loud sigh, watching the smoldering wreck of his barn as though expecting something whole to emerge from the ruins.

"What if *I* called the sheriff?" Randall moved away from the tree and stood in front of Joe.

"What's the point?" Joe's eyebrows arched with the question. "What could Jesse Surratt do now?"

Randall nodded toward the barn. "How much you want to bet there's not an open can of gasoline in there someplace? What if Surratt proved it belonged to Merle Oakley?"

"How could he prove that?"

"I don't know." Exasperation made Randall's headache worse, and when he spoke again, he kept his voice low. "I don't know how they prove that kind of stuff. But they do."

Joe shook his head again. "Nobody can prove Merle set the fire. I ain't seen him around here. Have you?"

Randall wondered if his neighbor was foolish enough to believe his trail of problems with nails and sugar and fire led anywhere other than Stella Oakley's husband. "Merle wouldn't have to take the road to get in here. There's logging roads all over these hills." Randall's headache was awful, and he thought about going to the house to ask Delia for aspirin. "A fire is serious. Aren't you worried about what he'll try next?"

The little smile appeared on Joe's face again. "I kind of meant to build a new barn anyway." He lifted his stump to point toward the ruined building. "Wonder if there's anything to salvage. Underneath I mean. Reckon a man could rake anything out from below the ashes?"

"I don't know." The roof had collapsed. It lay over the wreck of the barn like a metal shroud, still glowing red in places. "Maybe when this cools down." Randall fished in his pocket for keys and remembered he'd left them in the truck. "I'll come down in the morning and help you look."

Joe nodded, his eyes focused somewhere far away.

Randall drove home, and in bed told Mildred Joe's barn was a total loss. But he didn't tell the rest of what he and Joe talked about. If Mildred went to church the next morning, all she wanted to know about Joe Caudill and Merle Oakley would be whispered in the pews, between hymns. Mildred might be aggravated, once she realized Randall had known more than he said, but she'd get over it.

After the whiskey, and the excitement of the fire, Randall expected to fall asleep quickly, but an hour after he lay down he was still awake. Images of Stella Oakley floated behind his closed eyes.

Men had been nervous around Stella since she was fourteen. She'd kept her figure after four children, and if there was makeup on her olive skin, or dye in thick black hair inherited from a Cherokee grandmother, the artifice was applied so skillfully it didn't show. Stella's brown eyes were what Randall really noticed.

Whenever he stopped at the I.G.A. where Stella was a cashier, as she gave him change Stella always looked in his face, not at the hand where she put the money. Anytime he was close to her Randall wondered what lived behind eyes so bright, so clear, so fearless.

Before he went to sleep Randall was embarrassed by mind-pictures crowding his imagination. He was thinking about Stella and Joe Caudill in bed, wondering if she was bothered by the missing arm.

His face flushed hotly in the darkness, and he was glad Mildred was snoring faintly. He had the idea his feverish blush would be visible even with the lights turned out.

He was a long time finding sleep.

The next morning Mildred didn't rouse Randall for church. He woke to an unnatural quiet and wrapped himself in a terrycloth robe before padding off to the kitchen. Randall finished one cup of coffee before turning away from the windows facing his own barn. The fire was still with him, a sour reek of smoke and ash rising off his skin.

Losing a barn would be a rough blow. Randall had no idea what all was in his, what was stored in loft corners, stashed in stalls where he used to keep calves. Joe Caudill would be mourning newly discovered losses months after an insurance check marked the incident settled and done.

Randall was looking forward to a hot shower, then remembered his promise to assist in salvaging whatever was left from Joe's barn. He found the clothes he'd worn at the fire and dressed while drinking a second cup of coffee.

When he arrived at Joe's, his neighbor was already working, using a spud bar to pry back the collapsed tin roof. The blackened metal rolled in on itself as Joe levered it back with the spud bar and the weight of his body. When two or three square yards below it were exposed, the one-armed man poked at the wreckage as far as he could reach.

Things Joe thought might be saved were set aside, a pitifully small collection. There were some tools—wrenches mostly—in a small pile, and something shaped like a portable pump stood next to them. The hose had melted off the pump, if that was what it was. Randall doubted anyone would ever try to repair it.

"Hell of a mess," Joe grunted, leaning into the spud bar again. "Prob'ly not worth the trouble of digging around too much."

In an hour they rolled scorched tin off an approximate eighth of the concrete slab floor. Toward the middle of the concrete slab there was more to salvage than at the edges. The falling roof had smothered flames in the center of the conflagration. It was messy work though. Fire hoses had effectively soaked everything, and when Joe suggested a break their hands and faces were blackened and grease streaked.

"You didn't call Surratt did you?" Joe asked when they both had cigarettes lit in the shade of the big yard oak.

Randall shook his head. "Should've, though."

Joe squatted on his haunches, his back against rough bark. "It'll work out."

"You're making a mistake," Randall said. "For whatever that's worth."

"I put the dogs in the basement," Joe told him, as though Merle

55

Oakley was forgotten. "I need to get a place set up for them soon as we're done here. If they mess up her laundry room Delia's gonna be pissed for a month."

After smoking they went back to rolling up the old roof, stopping only when Delia Caudill brought a pitcher of iced tea outside. Even then they paused only long enough to drink a tumbler apiece before going back, taking turns leaning on the spud bar.

Delia stood on the back porch, the pitcher of tea left on the steps. Whenever Randall glanced her way she was watching, a tight grimace of a smile playing over her face from time to time.

Soon Joe and Randall approached the beginning of the fire, finding more things to salvage below the collapsed barn roof. Where the tin roof peaked like a blanket over a body they discovered a hay rake, useable with a little cleaning, and a sledgehammer with a nearly intact wooden handle. Joe's collection of items worth saving grew considerably.

But their work brought them to a place where destruction worsened steadily. A crowbar, too hot to pick up with bare hands, was twisted and warped, and less substantial metal objects were reduced to molten shapelessness. Over it all lay a heavy petroleum reek. The gas can was against the edge of the concrete foundation, one side blown out by the explosive force spewing fire through the barn. Looking at what had been a five gallon jerry can, Randall understood why there'd been no hope of controlling the fire, once it started.

When he spoke, Randall kept his voice low, because Delia was still watching from the porch. "Jesus, Joe, this has *got* to go to the sheriff."

Joe shook his head. "No it doesn't."

"I *told* you there'd be something left to show how Merle started your barn to burning." Randall almost spat the words, forgetting Delia for the time being.

Joe looked away from Randall, toward the house. "That's *my* gas can." His voice was a near whisper.

The words were like a foreign language Randall didn't quite understand. "What?" he asked.

Joe wasn't looking at Randall at all, was in fact staring beyond him, as though Randall had already gone. "How much of it was *you*? How much of it?"

Delia had left the porch to stand where an outside wall once rose. "Why?" she said, and her soft, nearly inaudible voice broke. Delia glanced at Randall, then began again. "Why did everyone think Merle's the only one who'd get angry? Why is that?"

Joe didn't answer.

Randall moved away from the Caudills, left them facing one another over the ruined building. He climbed into the cab of his truck, and watched Joe's face.

If Joe had an answer to Delia's question, his lips didn't form it until after Randall turned his truck around and headed home.

A Ride Across Open Water

Ice rattled as Paul Fitch leaned over the cab of his pickup truck, fumbling in the cooler for another beer. Snapping the can open, he dried his fingers on the knee of his work pants and glanced into the rearview mirror. An arcing wake marked the ferry's progress across Colley Bay, light from Burnham's Island chopped into dancing shards of color.

Raising his eyes a few degrees, Paul watched the island recede, winking neon pooled like a melted rainbow by the boardwalk. At Burnham's opposite end, the old lighthouse on North Point—a relic in an age when the smallest fishing boats carried radar—strobed a bar of stark white light across the darkness.

"Goddamnit, Bea." Paul's whispered words seemed loud in the pickup's cab, though he wasn't angry. He was frightened, but he suspected anger would make more sense.

At five o'clock Paul had walked through empty silence filling his house like a bad smell. He knew Bea had run away before the front door closed. The terse note taped to the refrigerator was confirmation, not the announcement she intended.

Twice in the week before she left, he came home to find his wife sleeping on the sofa, an empty glass that smelled of bourbon on the floor. Both times a pink and blue baby book, purchased the afternoon a doctor confirmed Bea's pregnancy, was on her lap. Paul's memory still held whole paragraphs from pamphlets and articles about Sudden Infant Death Syndrome.

A few months after the baby's death, he brought his wife to Burnham's Island. Paul worked in his father's construction company, immersing himself in brute labor he thought he'd left forever. For weeks at a time he was only marginally aware they lived on an island, unless Bea suggested riding the ferry.

Sometimes they stayed on the mainland long enough to have dinner. More frequently, Bea was content to remain on the pedestrian deck, waiting for the return trip. She loved the forty minute ride across open water. Pointing to the boardwalk, low on the horizon, she'd murmur "It's so *lovely*, Paul. Isn't it beautiful?" in the eliding Louisiana accent she never lost.

Before Bea showed Paul the island and ferry through Southern eyes, the boat was no more romantic than a bus ride, Burnham's Island only a place to live. He missed her reminder it was beautiful. She'd have been angry about the cooler of beer in the truck, though.

Paul expected to find Bea on the mainland, at the home of a woman she met while taking classes at the junior college. He'd copied the address from a list in the telephone book. Bea hated driving at night, and would save the real running away for morning.

He opened the cab door far enough to slip outside, careful not to bump an adjacent vehicle. A blue haired matron, clutching her steering wheel as though helping guide the ferry, pursed disapproving lips at his beer can.

At the stern, Paul leaned against the rail and stared into the boil and churn of the vessel's twin screws, wind ruffling his hair. Raising the can to his lips, he drank until it was empty, then pitched it into a nearby trash can.

The secret thought came.

He pushed it away, it came back.

Paul never saw the ferry's wake without fantasizing a leap into it. There was a siren attraction to the deadly thrash and splash at the stern. He forced himself to look further behind, at calmer water.

After they left their daughter in a cemetery outside Baton Rouge, Paul rode the ferry for hours, every day for a week. He spent those days poised over the wake. He thought about Bea, if he jumped. The ache of imagining her alone, among people she still called Yankees, saved his life.

Paul turned from the rail, opened a door to stairs leading to the upper deck passenger lounges. A slim and tall young woman stopped her descent as though striking a barrier. For a piece of time the girl stared at him from the landing, then turned and reversed her course.

She was like a deer, slim neck stretched like a running doe, sandaled feet slapping steel stairs until carpeting on the upper deck muffled the rhythms of flight.

At the top of the stairs Paul pushed through another door, into the lounge area. Noise from the ferry's engine faltered, caught again briefly, and died. Overhead lights flickered and were dimmer than before. Beneath the low wattage glow passengers rustled uneasily, engine vibrations beneath their feet suddenly stilled.

Two men in orange deckhand coveralls shoved through the crowd and marched the length of the lounge. They kept their eyes focused straight ahead, ignoring passengers who tried to attract their attention.

Before the ferrymen escaped, a fat man put his hand on the shoulder of one. "What's happened?" he asked. "Why'd we stop?"

The deckhand paused, but only for a moment. "A little engine trouble. Nothing to worry about." Then both crewmen slipped through the exit and were gone.

Paul recognized the uncertainty in the deckhand's voice. They were the notes his own voice carried, when there were problems on a job customers who knew nothing of construction couldn't understand. Like one of Paul's customers, the fat man nodded uncertainly before moving toward the tiny bar at one end of the deck, where drinks could be purchased at inflated prices.

Paul wished he could find the young woman he'd frightened on the stairs, explain there was no reason to be afraid of him. The wish meant he was drunker than he meant to be.

He turned back to the stairs. On the vehicle deck, he found his pickup truck and dug in the cooler for another beer. Breaking it open, he drifted back to the rail and looked into the night. Temptation still beckoned below the transom, though the black water stretching to the island was calm.

The ferry's lost momentum removed any hint of a breeze and Paul shucked off his jacket, draped it across the rail. Behind him, talk buzzed from nervous drivers, pacing beside their cars. Conversation was usually difficult on the automobile deck, only a few steps from engine room din. In the unnatural quiet, Paul believed he could hear a whisper, from one end of the ferry to the other.

The mainland, a blurry course of white light low on the horizon, was closer now than the island. Paul wondered what words would fit, when he found Bea. Until that moment, he'd thought only about catching her, had given no thought to what he might say.

There was movement in the darkness. One of the crew, orange coveralls folded into a bundle held under an arm, stepped to the rail. "My shift don't start for another hour," he explained to Paul's curious stare. "Put these on now, I'll have to answer the same. questions over and over."

Paul raised his beer and emptied it. "Are we going to be out here long?"

"That's one of those questions." The deckhand grinned as he lifted one foot and rested it on the rail. "Diesels quit if you don't maintain 'em." He lit a cigarette and shrugged. "Johnson, the engineer? He mostly spends his shift reading magazines."

The man leaned forward and spat over the rail. "They called for a tug." The embered end of his cigarette glowed when he put it back to his mouth. "Might be a while getting here, but it'll take us back in."

Paul stepped toward his truck, then turned to face the ferry crewman again. "Want a beer?"

"Wouldn't have a job if they caught me with it." The crewman grinned again. "Nice offer though."

At his truck Paul thought about getting in the vehicle, but the cab seemed confining in the humid darkness, even with windows open. Retracing his steps to the railing, he stood near the crewman, and raised his eyes to the throw of stars over the water. "If you have to take a long boat ride, this is a good night for it."

The man nodded. "It's good you ain't in a hurry." He gestured at passengers milling around their vehicles. "Another fifteen minutes, most of them will be acting like a little delay has ruined their lives."

"I'm chasing my wife," Paul blurted, surprising himself. He decided he wouldn't drink any more beer. He took a deep breath and exhaled loudly.

"Know where she went?"

"Bea's got a friend." Paul sipped from the beer can. "A woman, lives near Crown Point."

"That ain't too far." The man leaned his elbows on the rail and flipped the cigarette into the wake. "When you get there, don't do nothing foolish, get the police called."

The can he held was half full, but Paul dropped it into the trash anyway. Beer didn't taste good anymore. "We just need to talk."

The public address system crackled and a tinny voice called crew members to the wheel house. The man next to Paul unrolled his coveralls and stepped into them. "Shift starts early, looks like."

Paul watched him walk away and looked toward the shore again. The lights were fainter, as though the ferry was drifting toward open sea. He strolled back to his truck, where the dashboard clock showed a quarter to eleven, his normal bedtime.

The brief period of wakefulness after he and Bea lay down together was Paul's favorite moment of any day. Lying against Bea's warmth was sanctuary, a place nothing outside could touch. When the alarm went off at six a.m., they were nearly always still nestled together.

Paul moved the cooler to the floor, stretched across the seat and fell into a fitful doze.

In a dream he was working on a roof, the shingles slippery as wet ice. The job was finished, and someone was there to take him home, sounding the horn over and over, impatient for Paul to come down. In the dream, he felt guilty about making them wait.

Paul eased toward a ladder at the eave, steps cautious and tentative, but he slipped anyway. The ground seemed far away, progress toward the roof's edge very slow. Paul woke as his feet slid past the eave, the sickening sensation of skidding toward an abyss still with him when he opened his eyes.

Through the windshield, where there had been a watery expanse and a star dusted sky, he saw gray emptiness. The ferry's fog horn bellowed into the cloudy expanse like a lovesick sea serpent, the same rhythm as the impatient signal in his dream. Paul rubbed his eyes, massaging the ache behind them.

In the glove compartment he found a bottle of aspirin. A paper coffee cup was on the floor, and he dipped enough cold water from the cooler to swallow three pills. Hoping fresh air might ease the throbbing inside his head, he left his truck.

Ten paces from the pickup, dense fog blurred the vehicle's outline. Another ten and Paul couldn't see it at all. The figure of the crewman he'd spoken with earlier formed in the mist, talking to another orange clad worker. "Gonna be a while getting to your wife," the crewman said.

"What happened?" Paul asked.

The man shook his head. "Big night for engine trouble. Tug bent a shaft, and before they got another one out, the soup rolled in." Diesel engines rumbled in the distance, muffled by the fog. Paul stared toward the sound, seeing nothing.

"Coast Guard," the crewman explained. "Got a cutter out there, keeping other traffic away." The man took off his billed cap and scratched his head. "Not that there's much moving in a fog like this one."

"Think I'll go check the lounges," the other crewman said. "Last time I was there, some guy was saying we'd be in life rafts before daylight. Had a pair of grandma types all worked up till I made him hush." The man moved into the haze, swallowed up after half a dozen steps.

Paul watched the fog for a while, his mind empty. The murk looked so thick and tangible he should feel resistance as wind and current pushed them through it. His head throbbed, his stomach was rolling from too much beer and no food. More than anything in the world, Paul wanted to climb into bed with his wife, feel familiar curves against his belly as he drifted off to sleep.

Moments later the sound began, a faint, sibilant whisper. The Coast Guard cutter drifted close, drowned the whisper in engine rumble, but when its diesel rhythm faded, the sound was there again, a bit louder.

Paul heard rushing water, waves breaking into high surf. The sound was frightening. It didn't matter the ferry carried radar, or had the cutter there to guide it, they were drifting toward a beach. In his mind he saw the ferry break apart on black rocks. He stared into the fog, hoping to see lights, some indication of where they were.

"Whales." The crewman stepped closer. "That noise is whales. It's their breathing. If they were closer, and the wind was right, you could smell them. They got a terrible stink to their breath."

"Whales," Paul echoed. He'd lived on the island most of his life without ever thinking about whales being in the bay.

"Only hear 'em late at night." Leaning over the rail, the crewman spat into the wake. "Lately it's three grown ones and a baby. I think the young one is why they're here. Easier to find something to eat close in, maybe." He shrugged. "And there's big sharks in big water. Safer here, for the youngster."

The man moved away from the rail and stuck his hands in his coveralls' deep pockets. "Think I'll go see what the word is on that tug."

The sound of breaking surf moved in the night, until it sounded from dark emptiness to the left. Or perhaps the ferry drifted. Without seeing stars or lights it was hard to know what moved and what didn't.

Paul stared at the night. If Bea got away from him, he'd find her at the cemetery in Baton Rouge.

He thought about whales, and hoped the young one was safe.

WILLARD'S GOT A PROBLEM

Me and Willard are Navy retreads. Both of us left the service after one hitch, and wound up wearing uniforms again. I drove a truck while I was out, but I think Willard went to college someplace. Some of the weird things he says sure sound like he's been to college.

Like, when I tell him I'm back in the Navy because I couldn't find work anyplace in the whole blessed state of Kentucky, Willard says that's an excuse. He claims the real reason I'm in Uncle Sugar's Canoe Club again is I wanted to see the Southern Cross one more time, shining on the Pacific horizon like God's own running lights. Either that or I missed watching whales play in the North Atlantic.

All I know is nobody was hiring between Louisville and Ashland, and in another six years I'll retire on half pay. That's what's real to me, not the Southern Cross and whales.

I like Willard, except when he makes trouble over some sad eyed woman. Willard has problems with married women who aren't happy. Let me tell you about last Saturday night.

The oiler we're stationed in had been out for two weeks, letting some R.O.T.C. cadets and a few reservists get a little sea duty, and we pulled into a town up the coast for a day or two of rest. When the Officer of the Deck announced liberty call, me and Willard headed for a bar we know, a blue jeans and draft beer kind of place the young kids mostly stay out of.

While a country band set up to play, me and Willard argued about small ships and aircraft carriers. I say since you got to spend time at sea anyway, destroyers or frigates, where you know everybody in the crew, are the best part of the Navy. Willard says only someone who likes throwing up on a regular basis will roll around on a tin can when a bird farm is a big steel island not even a hurricane can move.

It's an argument nobody's ever going to win, but passes time easier than remembering how Liz and the kids moved back to her mother's while I was overseas last year. Or weird reasons for being back in the Navy. After a pitcher or two of beer Willard can talk your ears numb about the Southern Cross and whales.

Right after the band started its first song two couples came in and headed toward the back part of the bar, which was unusual. I guess they hadn't been there before. This particular saloon has two bars. One's at the front, and couples generally stay up there.

In the back, women sit in giggly groups of two or three, around shaky little tables. Men drink beer at the bar, trying to find the nerve to talk to somebody at one of those tables. Most everyone in the back looks to have had conversations with a divorce lawyer or two, somewhere along the line.

Willard watched the two couples settle in, eyeing one of the women especially close.

She was pretty, even if her hair was too short. She had dark brown eyes, a wide soft mouth, and a woman's body instead of that little girl look females don't know they're better off losing. She sat next to a man I took to be her husband. They had on rings anyway.

The husband flirted with the lady from the other couple, in one of those "Why am I with this one when that one is so nice?" moods. The other lady's husband seemed bored, with the flirting husband and the woman he took to be so nice.

Willard drank beer and watched, smoking cigarettes and grinning. His eyes never left the short haired lady, and I knew what he was thinking.

"Don't get started," I told him.

"Just looking," Willard answered.

"She's married," I pointed out.

"Big deal," Willard answered. "Her husband doesn't seem to know *he* is."

Willard was right. The guy was a great example of all the things married men do when they're beer stupid. He smiled and nodded at anything the other lady said, though I'd've bet a pitcher of beer he couldn't remember five words of it. While he showed his teeth and hung on every word, his wife was off to herself, left out of the conversation altogether. Suddenly she said, "Say something nice about *me*, Thomas."

Thomas ignored her, but directly she leaned across the table, blocking his view of the other woman. "Say something nice about *me*," she said again, like it was a dare. That time her voice was loud enough people at other tables turned around, wondering if something interesting was about to happen over there.

The room was a shade quieter when Thomas finally looked at his wife. He was wearing a mean grin, the kind of look Liz had when she joked about finding another man if I spent another six or eight months at sea. "You're putting me on the spot, Dorothy," he said. And turned back to the other lady.

"Somebody *ought* to put him on the spot," Willard said.

"Leave it alone," I told him. "What is it with you and married women?"

When the band started to play Willard stood up. "I believe I'll ask that one to dance," he said.

"Leave it alone," I told him, but Willard acted like he didn't hear. "Come back and sit down," I called, louder. "I'll get us another pitcher." It was too late. Willard was already at that table, leaning toward Dorothy.

I've drunk enough beer with Willard to know exactly what he would say while they waltzed. He'd look down at her, all dreamy eyed, and whisper, "For years I asked Santa Claus to bring you for Christmas. How come you never showed?"

"You're a wonderful dancer," he'd say. Willard tells them they're wonderful dancers no matter what. I heard him say it once to a lady who moved like she had on cement panties and lead slippers. "God your eyes are lovely," Willard would say.

I have yet to see a female not enjoy Willard's trashy talk. The band played a waltz, a two-step, then another waltz, and Dorothy looked to be having a good time. When it's just me and him talking,

Willard sounds pure hillbilly, but with women he uses a deep South mush-mouth voice.

Once he gets going good Willard turns words I can't say with a straight face into flowery stuff women love. He talked Dorothy into another dance, then took her off to the front bar for a while.

Willard bought her a drink, and while they sat there, I know he was saying things like "If someone hasn't been telling you every day of your life you're beautiful, you've been hanging out with the wrong crowd."

If Dorothy admitted that no, she didn't hear it every day, Willard would raise his eyebrows and ask, "What about your husband?," showing with a sad shake of his head what a raw deal he thought she was getting.

In a little while they were dancing again. Willard spun Dorothy across the floor and kept his eyes locked on hers, looking grateful as a starved pup at dinner to be touching her hands and twirling her around. During the next waltz there wasn't much daylight showing between them neither.

I don't like watching Willard play his little game. It makes me wonder what Liz was up to while I was overseas, if you know what I mean.

I finished a beer and thought about leaving Willard with Dorothy, only we'd split the cost of a cab and I didn't want to pay a whole fare back to the ship by myself. I was wondering if there were any other sailors in that end of town, looking to share a taxi, when I noticed Thomas was mad and looking mean as a wet cat.

The other couple had disappeared, and he was left with four dirty glasses and an ashtray that needed emptying. The little table didn't have room for his elbows, so Thomas leaned back in his chair and glared around the room.

He kept a close watch on the dance floor, like if he didn't, Dorothy and Willard would slip off to the front again, but when the music stopped she came back to the table. Willard trailed behind and came over to the bar, a toothy grin stretched across his face. Dorothy's face was flushed when she sat down next to Thomas, who started to ignore her all over again.

Willard emptied a glass of warm beer and refilled it from the second pitcher I'd paid for. "Doesn't anybody but me say anything nice to married women?" he asked, looking across the beer like he actually expected an answer.

I tried to talk sense to him. "Her old man's pissed. Leave it alone before something happens," I warned. "Stay here, drink beer and keep away from them people."

Willard nodded, so I told him, "I'm going to go dance."

I looked around until I found a lady who sort of reminded me of Liz. I can't seem to get used to dancing with anyone who isn't her size. Me and that lady were trading names and the usual things when I noticed Willard waltzing Dorothy again.

"I'm *not* hitting on you," he said as they danced past. "I don't get involved with married women."

The odd part of it is, Willard *doesn't* get involved with them, never takes them to a motel or nothing like that. Half the time he even lies about his name, so they can't track him down later.

When the music stopped Willard told Dorothy, "You have gorgeous eyes," and followed her back to Thomas. By then her grin was wide as Willard's. Willard says an unhappy woman's smile is the prettiest thing he's seen since Mama proved he wasn't going to be a bottle baby.

When I got back to our pitcher Dorothy was getting all the attention from Thomas she could handle. "Through with your boyfriend?" he sneered, loud enough anybody could hear. "Ready to go home?"

"You don't have to talk like that," Dorothy said.

"Talk anyway I want." Thomas stood up, unsteady on his feet, grabbing Dorothy's arm and pulling at her.

"He's a pissant," Willard muttered as they went by us.

"Well he's *her* pissant," I said. "Come on, let's find somebody to dance with." Across the floor Dorothy was trying to jerk away from Thomas, like his hand was hurting her arm.

Willard stood up, and his smile was gone.

"Don't get mixed up in what isn't even a little bit your business," I called after him, but Willard stomped off in their direction. After a couple seconds I followed.

By the time I got to the door Thomas had Dorothy outside, half dragging her toward a car.

"Knock it off, you asshole!" Willard yelled.

Thomas had enough drinks in him, when he turned around, he nearly tripped himself.

Willard took a step forward. "She didn't do anything wrong."

Thomas told Willard to mind his own fucking business.

"Let go of her arm," Willard ordered.

I stood behind him, hoping Thomas didn't have a gun in his car, that the Shore Patrol was busy someplace else.

Thomas let go of Dorothy and took a half step toward us. As long as guns and knives stayed out of the deal, I wasn't worried. Willard can take care of himself. I wondered if he'd let Thomas throw even one punch before decking him.

Then I saw something moving.

From the easy way Dorothy swung her purse, I figured there wasn't much in there besides Kleenex and loose change, but when it connected, Willard dropped like she had a brick hid in among the nickels and dimes. "Get in the car, Thomas," Dorothy said, and he did.

I knelt down and saw Willard wasn't really hurt, just knocked stupid by what he hadn't seen coming. When I looked up, Dorothy was smiling as she steered the car away from the curb.

Willard laughed for a long time after I told him how happy she looked, driving away.

I've been trying to figure out what he thought was funny.

If you ask *me*, I believe Willard's got a problem.

Junior Blevins

Pop started complaining about an extra memorial service while we were still in a hospital lounge, waiting for a hearse to come and get Mom. He said if we did one night of visitation after we got her back to Kentucky, anyone who really cared would be there. Adding a night in Indiana would only make people feel like they had to show up in both places.

Until I called a few funeral homes and found out how much it would cost, we'd all agreed that before we took our mother home, there'd be a memorial service in the town where she died. My sister Lena knew as well as I did Pop was worried about money, not aggravation for relatives he hardly ever talked to. She didn't argue though.

My brother Troy sat away from the rest of us and didn't say nothing. I could tell he was disappointed though. I think he was looking forward to showing off for his real estate buddies how tore up with grief he was, something like that.

By Wednesday none of us was sorry we did what Pop wanted. A mortuary room where the best part of our family was laid out in a copper colored box, the air thick with the stink of dying roses, was as bad a place as I ever been. A second night of dead flowers and a coffin would've made us all crazy.

Great Aunt Ruby showed up with two daughters for escorts. Except for Ruby, who doesn't stand but an inch or two over four foot, the women in that family are big stout things. They got blocked right away by people who didn't notice a little old lady trying to get to the coffin.

After a minute's pause, maybe not even that long, Aunt Ruby sailed right on through the crowd, leaving the daughters behind. I couldn't really see Ruby, just this empty space moving through the shoulder-to-shoulder turn-out. Ruby was almost out of that mob before I saw how she did it.

Ruby'd brought a heavy cane to lean on, and while she walked, swung it like a pendulum. Every time that cane banged some big man's ankles, he frog-jumped out of her way. It was funny, and when Ruby heard me laughing out loud she smiled and winked at me. It was the first thing I'd had to laugh about in a long while.

As I walked her to the casket Aunt Ruby told me about being there the day Mom was born. "I pinned the first diaper onto your mommy she ever wore," Ruby said. She meant to tell more but Lena come and got me. The Church of God preacher wanted to talk to us.

I left Ruby with Pop, who wasn't about to follow a minister into a little room where he'd have to talk about details of the service. It was like he was pretending there wasn't going to *be* a funeral the next day, that the mob in the mortuary was just another family reunion, only out of season.

Lena, Troy and me sat with Reverend Carlyle for almost an hour. I told him Mom wouldn't have wanted a service full of religion, or an hour of sin and salvation preaching. Carlyle wrinkled his face when he realized he wouldn't save any souls at our mother's funeral, but he nodded and said he understood.

Lena mentioned a piece of Bible verse she wanted him to read, and the preacher recited the whole thing and more.

All Troy wanted to talk about was what a hard worker Mom had been. Troy didn't seem able to hush, once he got going.

About the time we came out of our meeting with the preacher, one more old timer I didn't know showed up. By then I'd faced two or three dozen strangers, explained who I was, stood beside them in front of that awful open box. I wouldn't have given another unfamiliar face a second thought if it hadn't been for the way my father acted.

Some of Mom's kin treated her badly, the last few years she lived. If they showed up, Pop wanted them met at the door and told their sympathy was not welcome. Then he wanted them *gone*. Watching my father's face, I wondered if the skinny old man in a gray suit was some mean tempered cousin. If so, I'd do better at evicting him than my brother or sister.

For as long as I can remember I've been the one in our family who doesn't much care what anybody else thinks. It bothers the rest of them some. A lot really, but it's a useful attitude to have once in a while. If there were unwanted relatives to toss out of the funeral parlor, not caring whose feelings got hurt would work better than Troy's stagy "look at me" grief, or Lena's tolerant exhaustion.

Besides, I was in a mood for an eviction.

At funerals I get to feeling what I guess is pissed off. I don't know what I'm mad at, whether it's God or something else, but I can't help thinking how unfair death is. No matter what comes before, the end of an old person's life is most of the time weeks and months of assorted insults and indignities. That's what I think about at funerals, the insults, not the life before them.

And I get mad.

Mom's finish was bad as any, and I wasn't yet over long nights of pain and crying that came before she died. Chasing someone who'd hurt Mom's feelings away from her coffin wouldn't've been a bit hard.

I meant to catch the old man before he got anywhere near Mom's casket, except Reverend Carlyle grabbed my arm and said, "I'd like to pray with you children before I go."

I come real close to laughing again. Lena, Troy and me carry right at a hundred and fifty years between us. The preacher wasn't much over forty, and him calling us "children" was almost as funny as Aunt Ruby's trick with her cane.

Reverend Carlyle had known Mom and Pop before they sold me the home place and left Kentucky, moved one more time to a factory town in Indiana. I never did understand why they did that, twenty years after finally coming home. They said it was to be closer to grandchildren, which didn't make a bit of sense. All but one of Lena's kids were grown, and Troy's were so mad about his divorce, they didn't want nothing to with any of the family.

Mom never was an actual member of his church, and when Carlyle agreed to preach her funeral, it was kind of a favor. I would have given him time for a few words even if my sister hadn't aimed slitted eyes at me over his shoulder. Lena wanted a prayer, with me standing there while it was prayed. Besides, Pop had already turned away from the tall stranger, wasn't looking hard at him anymore.

I let the preacher have his three or four minutes, but soon as he said the amens I pulled loose to check on that old man. It struck me as odd my father hadn't said anything to him. Pop loves talking to people from the old days, but instead of starting a conversation, he wandered off toward the smoking room at the back of the mortuary.

I eased through the crowd fast as I could, certain one of Mom's contrary kin had shown up after all. None of us had seen those people in years; I thought maybe Pop was acting funny because he couldn't decide whether or not he recognized this one.

I stood behind and a little to the left as the stranger stopped in front of the coffin. When the ones sitting in folding chairs looked over at us, I could tell some knew the man. Soon as Aunt Vonnie, one of Mom's sisters, glanced our way, her eyes went big as quarters. I took a step nearer to what I thought was a bullheaded cousin, but my sister moved in front of me.

"It's okay," Lena whispered. "I know who he is."

"And?" I asked.

"And I'll tell you later."

The man didn't stay more than five minutes, and left without stopping to speak to anybody. I followed him down the hall, through a door held open by a dead-eyed attendant wearing a shiny black suit. Outside, where the air didn't stink of stacked roses, I took a deep breath, let it out loud enough the skinny old man turned to look at me.

He smiled. "You're one of the kids."

I nodded and we shook hands. "I'm Roy Lee."

"You'd be Maude's eldest, then. I'm Junior Blevins." His lined face made two days of ache in my throat swell to near-choking me. For five or six hours I'd been surrounded by sad people with sad, leaking eyes. Junior Blevins was that and more; he looked broken.

"Maude and I were friends, a long time ago," he told me.

He stood there like he expected me to ask a question, but I only bobbed my chin up and down, no more able to talk than the stuffed toy Lena's youngest stuck on the window of my pickup, the week before Mom died. I stared past Junior Blevins at the Garfield hanging there, needing to look anywhere but into an old man's hurting eyes. Another ten seconds of seeing his pain and I'd be crying. I didn't want to do that until I was off by myself again.

When I didn't speak Junior Blevins smiled again before he walked off and climbed into a new Buick parked way down at the edge of the parking lot.

Being by myself to cry didn't happen for a while. After the visitation shut down, Lena came to the house, and Pop went to stay at his brother's. I reckon he knew me and Lena would spend time putting liquor between us and what all had gone on that day. A son who's bad to drink is hard enough for Pop to deal with. He can't hardly look at Lena when she's holding a whiskey glass.

I asked our brother if he wanted to come out and be with us, but Troy said no, he'd go on back to his motel room. His new wife Connie had worked hard at being nice, but I could tell she was glad she wouldn't see any more of us until morning.

Lena and me carried a bottle and two glasses onto the back porch, with a big jug of Pepsi and a kettle of ice. It felt good, sitting in the dark with nothing more complicated to do than keep a few ice cubes floating. I didn't know I could get so tired, smiling at people I barely recognized, watching for relatives who didn't belong anywhere near Mom.

"So," I said after a while. "Who's Junior Blevins?"

Lena closed her eyes, turning her face toward the cool air drifting off the ridge. I remember that breeze from every spring of my life. It has a taste as sweet and real as ripe melons. I don't care how much Lena hates coming back to Kentucky, how much she loves her life in Indiana, I bet she misses the taste of wind after sundown.

"Junior was Mom's old boyfriend."

"Well." I didn't know what to say to that. I don't think I'd've been more surprised if my sister said Mom turned Catholic on her death bed. "You're kidding," I said, more to break the quiet than anything else.

Lena shook her head. "Remember the car wreck story? About when Mom totaled a new Ford truck and a boy took the blame so Grandpa wouldn't whip her?"

Telling tales from when she was a girl, Mom could make anybody laugh out loud. At the mortuary a few old people had talked about how much everybody loved her in the old days, how pretty she was, how everybody looked forward to having her come around.

"Junior was the boy?"

Lena nodded, took a drink from her glass, then a hit off one of the long brown cigarettes she smokes. She hates it she never can find those things in the local stores if she runs out. "Tell you something else about him."

"What?"

"One time, he tried to get Mom to leave Dad."

Suddenly it wasn't just me and my sister sitting on the porch, getting a little drunk. We'd moved into something important, and I turned my chair to face Lena. "Was that when *something happened*? Is Junior what that was all about?"

Anytime Lena and me drink together, sooner or later we talk about *the time something happened*. Without the first clue to what *something* was, we know it happened, on account of all the changes that came afterward.

Mom stopped singing when she worked around the house, and didn't tell funny stories unless we begged her to.

Before *something happened*, Pop used to sneak up on Mom when she washed dishes. He'd surprise her with a pat on the rear end, and wrap his arms around her. Mom would jump at his touch, then settle in against Pop while he whispered things with his mouth close to her ear.

After *something happened* Mom went back to school and became a licensed practical nurse. Pop got a new job, fixing audio visual equipment for the school system, and for the first time in their lives they weren't poor. But Mom didn't sing, and they didn't touch one another when they thought us kids weren't looking.

"Is that what changed things? Junior showing up?"

Lena shook her head, and the ice kettle rattled when she picked it up. She didn't say anything until she'd made a fresh drink and had another cigarette lit.

"No. Junior came after that." Lena's face got thoughtful. "Reuben was three the year he came around, I think. Three or four. I was still in junior high school when *something happened*."

Reuben was my sister's oldest, twenty-two by the time Mom's cancer was diagnosed. If he was three when Blevins came courting Mom, I was already overseas with the Navy and wouldn't have known anything about it.

"Junior lived in Detroit," Lena said. "And his wife died. He waited a while, and then he came to get Mom."

I swallowed the last of my drink, poured another and tossed off half. It was my third to Lena's one. A couple more and the bourbon would stop tasting good, but by then I wouldn't care. "Did Pop know about it?"

"I don't know that Mom told him." My sister leaned forward, flicked ashes off the cigarette and watched their drift, all the way to the yard. "But he had to have figured out something was going on."

"What do you mean?"

"He couldn't have missed it, after the way Mom started acting. She was wearing make-up, using perfume, I don't know what all."

Pop *would* notice that. My folks got past their old time religion while I was in high school, but hating whiskey, not wearing make-up and other Pentecostal habits die hard. I couldn't help grinning, picturing my mother putting on lipstick, or dabbing perfume behind her ears. Lena giggled, and for a little while it was like Mom was with us, telling a story.

"And she started slipping out at night without telling anybody where she was going," my sister said.

"No kidding?"

"No kidding," Lena echoed.

"How come you never told me about this?"

"I didn't know about it until six months ago. Remember when Mom stayed at my house for two weeks?"

I nodded. After her third layover in the hospital Mom needed somebody with her full time, and instead of making trips across town Lena took her home, kept her there till she was stronger.

"That's when Mom told me about it." My sister sighed. "Junior hung around town the better part of a week, trying to talk Mom into going back with him. I sort of remembered him after she told me what he'd been doing there. I met him at least once but I had no idea about the rest of it."

"Was he crazy or what?"

"I don't think so." Lena paused two or three heartbeats. "Mom told me she almost went with him."

"Good lord." The story my sister told was a whole lot for me to get hold of, and I needed to put it down for a little bit. Standing up, I stretched, and then stepped down off the porch. "Make me another drink, will you? I gotta water a patch of grass."

Lena made a face, but took my glass and as I walked off into the darkness, I could hear the ice rattling down into it.

Every man I know who has his own land needs to stand outside to pee once in a while, and every woman I know hates it that we do. On the other side of the garage I did what I needed to in the shadows. When I was done I spent some time just looking up, studying an endless complication of stars.

My mother was dead.

And she'd nearly left my father, twenty-some years ago.

I wasn't sure which was harder to believe.

When I went back to the porch Lena and me had a couple more drinks before she decided to go stay with Pop. Not too long after, three of my nephews showed up and said they wanted to sleep at the house that night. I took the bottle inside, and me and the boys talked across the kitchen table till way past midnight. I told stories about their grandmother, but not the one about Junior Blevins.

He didn't come to the funeral. All the time Reverend Carlyle preached, I thought about what Lena said before leaving my house. "I wish Mom had gone with that man," she told me. "Maybe she'd have been happy, you think?"

I didn't know.

Still don't.

I did one thing I'm kind of proud of, at the funeral. It was one of the few times in my life I've known the exact right words somebody needs to hear. At the end of the service, after everybody had filed by the coffin one last time and the lid was shut on the horrid thing, my nephew Reuben broke down, and it looked like he might not be able to finish being a pall bearer.

I walked over to him and put my mouth close to his ear. "You know your grandma loved you," I said. "And you know she appreciated everything you did for her, the last two or three years?"

Reuben turned big brown eyes at me and nodded.

"You ain't got but one more thing to do for her, son," I said. "Then it'll be over and done with. Just carry her the rest of the way and it'll be over."

Reuben straightened up, sucked tears and sobs someplace back inside himself, and the boy did well, the rest of the service.

I almost never know just the right thing to say, but I nailed it that time.

It rained for a week after we buried Mom, but the first dry day, I went back to the graveyard. Flower arrangements from the service had been thrown away, but an enormous wreath of fresh tulips had taken their place, over the low mound of naked dirt.

Tulips were Mom's favorites.

Looking down at the bright spring flowers, knowing who put them there, I remembered the haunted loneliness in my mother's eyes after *something happened.*

I thought about what Lena told me, what she wished Mom had done.

I thought about it a long time.

And then *I* wished she'd gone back to Detroit with Junior Blevins too.

TIMBER

Wednesday nights was "anger management group," which everybody in it called "mad class," in a trailer behind the mental health clinic. What we did there was play-act, something the Doc called "role playing." The last night I was there, right before Mary Parton tore up my life, the Doc set me and Toby Reynolds in chairs, out in the middle of the room, where we was to pretend Toby had cut me off at a parking space downtown.

The Doc started it off by asking "Now Mr. . . ." He had to look down at his book on account of never remembering my name. "Mr. Carter, how would you deal with a situation like this?"

I said, "There is so much parking downtown since the Walmart come in, what would be the point to making a big deal over one little space?"

"But what would you do if Mr. . . ." The only name the Doc ever remembered was Mary Parton's, so he had to peek at his notes again. ". . . if Mr. Reynolds cut you off when you were about to park?"

The truth was, if I found somebody cutting me off for a parking space I'd wonder what town I was in, 'cause it sure wouldn't be Midland. "I reckon I would talk to Toby about it," I said. The answer the Doc always looks for is when they get mad people need to talk.

"That's good," he said. "And what would you say to him?"

Mad class wasn't so bad when it was just setting on a metal folding chair and watching Mary Parton, the most interesting woman I ever seen. But nights the Doc put me to play acting, I couldn't help but think I'd like just once to put his lights out. But that is the kind of thinking which got me into mad class in the first place, so I settled down and begun what he wanted me to do. "I would go to Toby, and I would discuss it with him."

The Doc nodded. "What would you say?" he asked again.

"I would tell him if he didn't have no better sense than to cut somebody off for a parking space, he ought to keep his piece of shit Chevy off the road."

Toby give me the finger and said "Well fuck you too, Willford Carter. I reckon I can park any goddamn where I want to on a public goddamn road."

"Well even on a public road you don't need to drive like you mean to cause a wreck," I told him back.

"Mind your own goddamned bidness and let other people tend to theirs," Toby said. He was quiet a second or two and then added, "If you don't *know* how to mind your own bidness, I could maybe show you."

I looked over at Mary in time to see her reach up with one hand to move the hair away from her forehead. Looking into her eyes I once again got the feeling Mary knew more than anybody else in the room.

Including the Doc, who hardly ever put Mary in one of his role plays.

I play-acted getting out of my truck—even pretended to slam the door—and walked to where Toby was hogging that parking space. Bending over like I was leaning in a window I said, "You could get out right now if you think you got anything to show *me*."

Mostly, me and Toby was only trying to get on Dr. Fitzgerald's nerves. I say "mostly" because all them Reynoldses think way too much of themselves, and I wouldn't care a bit to show Toby he ain't such a big deal. I whipped his ass three times before we quit high school, and I could do it again.

Everybody was all the time pranking with the Doc, who hardly ever figured out we were joking around. It was comical when he got wound up tighter'n a two dollar watch, thinking some true anger might get loose in his trailer. I don't reckon he ever stopped to think a real fight would put me and Toby both in jail, and we wasn't about to let that happen.

Not over a pretend parking place anyway.

It took most of mad class for the Doc to show how he thought Toby and me was to act, if we was ever to argue over parking spots downtown. Which, unless the Walmart burns down, is as likely to happen as a certain bat moving to Detroit, and we go back to cutting trees.

The bat, which lives in our part of the National Forest and no place else, is why everybody who cut timber got laid off three years ago. After a year, unemployment checks run out, and there was nothing to do but file for other benefits.

The people that run them other benefits think their weekly check—nine and a half dollars less than unemployment—gives them the right to mess with your life. They decided I needed a GED diploma and enrolled me in classes without even talking to me about it.

I didn't care about their GED. Once we got back to cutting timber, it wouldn't make a fart in a windstorm's difference, and all I learned in their classes is I had forgot anything I ever knew about arithmetic.

And also about history.

Two weeks into my GED studying I got put into mad class. I had failed the history pre-test for the fourth time, and afterwards a snotty clerk called me a "displaced worker," said I ought to be grateful somebody was doing something about my ignorance.

The clerk ratted me out for offering to put a displaced number twelve boot up his ass as far as the ankle, which Judge Wallace called a threat. The judge also said it was either go to mad class or lose benefits, and pay a fine besides.

After we got done with parking spaces, the Doc made a speech about how it is often feelings of insecurity which make a person mad. He said we should learn to be ready to feel that way, so as to be prepared when it happened. He told us the same thing two or three different ways, using all kinds of words, but that's all I got out of it. The man's a fool for complicated talk and saying the same thing over and over.

Then he told Bessie Harper to stand with Lonnie Stevens and play-act being in a place where Lonnie asks Bessie to dance, and Bessie says "No." Both of them messed up right away, and when me and Mary looked at one another again, she winked at me.

The mental health people keep poor old Bessie doped up to the place she don't know more than a locust stump does about what's going on around her. Even without them pills, she'd likely do anything for a man who asked nice, and telling Lonnie she wouldn't dance with him was a tough thing for her to get hold of.

Lonnie was a hard nut to crack in that piece of play acting too. He's strong Church of God, and don't believe in dancing, didn't want to even pretend to do what his preacher takes for sin. But the pranking from me and Toby had used up all the Doc's patience, besides which you could tell he thought it was another joke, Lonnie calling it a sin to ask Bessie to dance.

The Doc decided to show he was by God in charge after all, and said if Lonnie didn't do as he was told, Judge Wallace would get a bad report on him in the morning.

For a man running classes on it, Dr. Fitzgerald don't understand a whole lot about people getting mad. When he gets stirred up, Lonnie's one of them hot-tempered runts who'll have a normal sized man beat half to death before the other feller even knows he's in a fight.

Lonnie got as red in the face as anybody can without having a stroke. For a time I figured the Doc was gonna find out about real anger management, and it would've been a hard lesson. But Lonnie finally did what he was told before Bessie forgot she was to say "No," and after she said it Lonnie fell down into a chair with his arms crossed, tapping one foot and watching the wall clock.

It was a pretty interesting mad class, and I'd a never guessed it was my last one.

All the time I was going to mad classes, Mary Parton made two silly hours every Wednesday night an easy thing to take. I liked watching how she moved, how she looked at all of us, and when she smiled everything seemed funny.

Mary moved away soon as she finished high school and lived someplace up in Illinois or Ohio till her mother got cancer. She come home for that, and would have been gone from Midland a long time ago, except for knocking hell out of a nurse two nights before her mama died.

They say what it was, the nurse didn't move fast enough with a morphine shot to suit Mary, and after getting her nose broke the nurse had Mary arrested for assault. Judge Wallace sent Mary to Doctor Fitzgerald's mad class, just like he did me and the others.

The Doc was even more out of place than Mary. Once when Patty Jo needed the truck to go to her sister's, she dropped me off a few minutes early. Smoking a cigarette outside, I heard through an open window what the Doc said on the telephone. He was telling somebody how awful it was, having to work here because he couldn't pay back some money he borrowed to go to school. "My office is a *trailer*, for god's sake," I heard him say.

It was a nice trailer though. From inside you'd never think you were sitting over wheels, and Dr. Fitzgerald's job don't look that hard. And you just know he makes more money running mad classes than anybody working in the woods ever did.

After the Doc let us go that night, I meant to head on home. If I hadn't stopped to light a smoke things might've been different. But fooling with my lighter gave Mary time to catch up and ask if I was in a big hurry.

Patty Jo was already in bed, or just about to get there, and looking at it that way, there didn't seem to be no need for me to rush off to the house. If it'd been anybody else, I *would* have gone on home, but if you've seen Mary, you know why I stayed out that night.

When she first come to mad class, Toby tried nicknaming Mary Parton "Dolly," but he quit when she looked at him real hard over it. She don't look nothing like the singer no way. Mary's real slim, and her dark brown hair's short as I ever seen on a woman. But it looks good. Mary don't wear much make-up neither.

Mary Parton's beautiful is what she is. Every time she moved I thought of hawks in high summer, soaring clean and easy, beautiful without ever thinking what they look like. Outside the Doc's trailer, that's how she strolled over to me, graceful as a hawk.

"Gimme a ride home?" she asked.

Mary didn't live but five or six blocks from the mad class trailer. Whenever Toby Reynolds offered her a ride, she always said she'd rather walk, even one night when it was raining. I wondered what she really wanted. Women like Mary don't ask guys like me for rides.

"Truck's across the street," I told her, but she was already walking to it.

"Nice ride," she said when she got settled in.

"Payments are high though," I admitted. That same afternoon some guy from the credit union had come to the house, said if I didn't get caught up, pretty soon somebody'd be by to take it back to the dealer.

"Can we go someplace before you take me home?" Mary wasn't asking, she was telling, but it seemed okay, the way she did it. "You know where the Big Perry fire trail is?"

"Work in the woods long as I have and you'll learn every one of them trails," I told her.

What the Forest Service calls "trails" are graded gravel roads running all through the National Forest. The government makes timber companies build them in case they need to get equipment and men to a fire in a hurry. If you know the way they run, you can get just about anyplace in Hawkes County, and hardly ever cross pavement. When I feel like getting out of the house and away from Patty Jo, I like to follow fire trails, see where all I wind up.

At the edge of town, by the Ashland mini-mart, Mary said, "Pull in for a second."

I sat hoping nobody'd notice whose truck she got out of. It wouldn't do for Patty Jo to hear I was driving around after mad class with Mary, or any other woman. But I wouldn't've cared if Toby Reynolds drove by in time to see her step down from my Dodge.

Mary come out with a Coke and ice, and once we were on the highway, reached into her big purse and pulled out a pint of Beam. She cracked the seal, took a double swallow and handed the bottle to me. Whiskey on my breath would mean two hours of bitching if Patty Jo smelled it. I let Mary's little hand hang there a while before I took the bottle and poured down a dose, chasing it with some of her Coke.

A mile or two out of town, Mary rolled down her window and it was fine how wind blew her short hair around. Till we got to the fire trail it was just passing the bottle and the Coke back and forth without talking. I drove and breathed perfume that smelled like lemons only not exactly, and wondered how it would feel to have one hand full of that hair

Mary Parton ain't like other women in Hawkes County. The times we were in mad class I studied a lot on how she was different, and never did work it out all the way. She's smart without being a smart-ass, never makes people around her feel dumb. Looking like she does, Mary can't help but make men feel awkward, but she never made me feel stupid.

She acts like *her* life is under control, while the rest of us are forever shoved around. Even the Doc, on account of owing money to somebody, has to live in a place he hates. Mary was smart enough to get loose from Hawkes County after high school, and was free in a way the rest of us weren't. When she laughs you hear freedom.

I heard it when she giggled and said, "You sure don't think much of Toby Reynolds, do you?"

"He's okay," I told her.

"Bullshit," Mary said. "That wasn't all pretend tonight. For a little while I thought you all were really gonna get into it."

See? Mary knows things nobody's explained to her.

I drove two thirds of the way to the end of the main fire lane, and then turned onto a rutted road we'd once pulled logs out on. It was an easy grade for my truck, but Crown Vics the county deputies drive couldn't follow. Me and Mary wasn't doing nothing wrong, unless you count drinking the whiskey, but them deputies are as bad to gossip as a bunch of Baptist widows.

I stopped the truck on a point jutting out over ten or twelve acres of clear-cut, and when the lights shut off, till my eyes got used to seeing by a sky full of stars, it seemed dark as a cave. The sky is why I like the fire trails at night.

Mary noticed it too. "Pretty," she whispered, handing over the pint.

Three or four jolts on the way from town had me feeling pretty good, so I drank more Coke than whiskey. I pointed and told Mary, "In daylight you could look down that way and see where we were cutting, right up to the time they made us stop."

Without looking where I pointed Mary asked, "You know Roy Robinson?"

"Worked with him some," I told her.

Roy run the skidder on our crew, but he's sloppy, knocks down twenty saplings to reach a log instead of going around the little trees. I don't like watching that.

"Roy's my second cousin," Mary said. "He claims you all ain't going back to work for a long, long time. Not till timber gets to be more important than bats."

I hadn't said it out loud, but I'd been thinking the same thing. My hands was softening, even the space between two fingers of my right hand, where one callous has been since I was sixteen. It's from jerking the starter cord on a chainsaw fifteen or twenty times a day. If I touched it with my thumb, the roughness was about gone.

When Mary offered another drink I thought about never again working in the woods, and took a *big* swallow. When I handed the Beam back to her Mary was looking at me in a way I recognized.

Most of the time I can drive a fence post with the end of an eighty foot oak, drop it right where I want it. But every now and then a cut tree will twist on you, and then there's no telling where it's gonna go. You know you have to jump, but you don't know which way.

That's how Mary looked at me, like I was a tree she was cutting and she didn't know which way I was gonna fall.

"Know Donnie Douglas?" she asked.

"Just who he is," I told her. Donnie's a car dealer, but there's a lot more to what he does than cars.

Patty Jo's brother's a contractor, and two, three years back put in a swimming pool for Donnie, then built a redwood deck all the way around the house. Randy says the day he give him the bill, Donnie glanced at it, and told him to wait right there.

Donnie went in the house and come out with a grocery sack full of hundreds, thirty-four thousand dollars loose in a paper bag. Randy'd never carried so much money in his life, said all the way to the bank he shook like he had a palsy. While she was counting the bills, the bank teller said, "Looks like you been working for Donnie Douglas."

Donnie moves a lot more out of eastern Kentucky than used cars, and everybody knows it ain't just pot, that he's got people making speed and other stuff for him. Way before the bank teller finished counting, Randy decided he wasn't going to do no more work for the man, ever.

"Do you know Donnie well enough to speak to him?" Mary asked.

"Not really."

"I do."

"You do what?"

"Know him to speak to." Mary took a big draw off her cigarette and blew smoke through the open window. "*More* than just to speak to, if you want to know the truth." When she turned around on the seat I could feel Mary's eyes on me, wondering which way I'd fall, which way she'd need to jump. "If I was to tell you something," she said, "Could you not tell about it?"

I knew I was fixing to get into something with Mary Parton I didn't want nor need, and I knew I couldn't stop it from happening. From the time she stepped into my truck I couldn't have stopped it. I could feel a bad thing out there, coming closer, but I couldn't stop it.

Off in the woods a dead limb snapped under a deer's hoof, and it sounded loud as a pistol shot in the quiet. The deer didn't stir for a long while, waiting for something awful to happen from stepping on that stick. In my truck I waited for a thing just as awful to come out of giving Mary Parton a ride home.

Neither one of us, me nor the deer, moved for a long time. I took a deep breath when I heard it moving downhill into the valley, probably surprised to realize it'd live to see daylight. Sitting next to Mary I didn't feel nearly so safe.

"Well could you?" she asked again. "Not tell ?"

I nodded. "You can tell me anything you want to," I said.

Mary shifted in the seat, pointing her knees in my direction. "When I started messing around with Donnie I didn't know he was married. Wasn't no ring on his finger." She reached over and tapped my left hand where it was wrapped around the steering wheel. "It's more honest when a man wears a ring like you do."

The stars made my wedding band shine. Patty Jo'd throw a fit if I ever took it off. I didn't want to talk about wedding rings though, and when I lit a cigarette I blew the smoke out real loud. Dr. Fitzgerald says that's a sign you're getting something off your chest without saying anything.

I hadn't yet done nothing wrong, but already knew I was going to.

"I got to get out of this shitty little town." Mary fidgeted some, and then said, "Tonight was my last night in that stupid class. I'd leave tonight if I had the money."

I sat easier, thinking Mary was leading up to me loaning her money, or giving her some. If I was working I might've handed over fifty or a hundred, then lied to Patty Jo about where it went, but the way it was, I barely had gas money to the end of the week. "I'm sorry, but I can't . . ." I started to say.

"What if I was to tell you that before tomorrow morning you could make a thousand dollars?" Mary asked. "And *I* could make a thousand, and be out of this town."

She was talking about doing something for Donnie Douglas. Maybe after we come out of the Doc's trailer I hoped Mary was taking me into the woods to get screwed. Maybe I didn't care why we went out there, maybe it was enough to just look at her, close enough to smell lemon perfume. I was in a place I didn't belong, and didn't care. I wanted to be there.

But the idea of doing anything for Donnie Douglas made me wish I was at home in bed.

Mary stopped looking at me like I was a tree about to fall. I was already down, and she hadn't had to jump out of the way after all.

"Let's go," she said in the dark. The bottle went back in her purse and she poured the rest of the Coke out the window. "You know where Donnie's sister lives?"

I wanted another hit of that bourbon, but didn't say nothing about it. "Up Dry Branch a ways," I answered.

"Donnie and them have serious money to pay people like us." Mary was almost whispering. "This could work out a whole lot better than cutting trees."

I knew Donnie Douglas—and anybody he was mixed up with— didn't mean nothing good for guys like me. I knew all that, but I didn't say nothing, just drove toward Dry Branch Road and wished I'd gone home after mad class.

When we got to Frieda Douglas's house Donnie was on the porch, waiting. Inside somebody was moving around, stepping in front of the windows every now and then. I wondered who they were, if they knew who *I* was. I started to pull in behind a dark Buick but Donnie motioned me to park off to the side.

"Wondered if you all were coming or not," he said, sounding about half-pissed. I almost made a joke about anger management, but the whiskey buzz had turned into a headache, and Mary didn't look like anything would make her laugh. "You tell him the deal?" Donnie didn't look at me.

Them benefits people never look at me neither, always aim their eyes behind or beside me, the way Donnie Douglas did. I stepped to the right and made him look at me. Donnie's face was even meaner when he smiled.

After that I didn't care where he looked.

"We drop the cars off in New Albany and get our money," Mary said. "That's all there is to it, right?"

Donnie nodded. "That's all." He motioned me over to the Buick. "You both got CB radios and a full tank of gas," he told me. "Don't lose sight of each other, and if something happens like a flat tire, anything like that, you let Mary know you've had to stop. There's a Union 76 across the river from Louisville. Somebody'll meet you there."

Donnie went back inside his sister's double-wide, and Mary and me was by ourselves again.

"Do I leave my truck here?" I asked.

"Donnie'll have somebody take it to your house," Mary answered.

I thought about writing a note for Patty so she'd know I was all right, but then she'd be even more worried. Once in a while, when I wind up passed out in somebody's car and don't get home till morning, Patty warpaths me for a day or two. She'd do more than warpath if she knew I was driving one of Donnie Douglas's cars to Louisville.

"Ready?" Mary asked. When I nodded she reached in her purse and tossed the whiskey bottle at me. "Go easy on that," she said. "You follow me, all right?"

I nodded again, and Mary climbed into a silver Taurus. By the time I got the Buick's seats adjusted and the mirrors fixed right, she was fifty yards gone. I was glad she headed into Mather County to pick up I-64 rather than going back through Midland. If anybody in town seen me driving that Buick, Patty'd hear about it for sure.

I only let myself have one drink every half hour, timing it by the clock on the tape player. And no matter how weird it sounds, especially after what happened, I wish I could redo that four hours to Louisville. Till we crossed the river into Indiana, I had the best time of my life.

We kept the CB radios on and talked back and forth the whole trip. Or mostly she talked and I listened. Telling about socking that nurse in the nose, Mary made it into a real funny story, even if it was also about her mama dying, and I laughed hard as I ever will.

And she had other funny stories about what all she'd done after leaving Hawkes County.

She'd done all kinds of things to make a living, and every one of them could make a television show. She even spent a year working as a topless dancer in Columbus, but what she told about it was funny, not dirty. I didn't know women in places like that make fun of men who lay dollars down in front of them, or that the men never guess they're being laughed at.

Once we hit the outskirts of Louisville Mary grew quiet, and I didn't laugh no more. It was two in the morning, but there was lots of traffic, not all of it semis. I wondered where all those people were going to or coming from so late.

Mary stayed right at the speed limit. I was most of the time able to keep near enough nobody cut in between us. Wasn't hard, because everybody wanted to pass us.

Crossing the bridge into Indiana Mary got on the radio again, and soon as she started talking I knew this was where things would go wrong. "Ever have to do something bad because somebody could *make* you do it?" It sounded like Mary was about to cry.

I couldn't think of nothing to say. My mind was empty as the whiskey bottle, and I couldn't think of nothing to fill it with.

"Sometimes you can't help what happens," she said.

Suddenly Mary Parton was flying away from me, red tail lights growing dim as the blue flashers coming up from behind got brighter, and nearer. I knew a whole lot, right at that moment, knew it so clear it was like a voice had been explaining things all the way from Hawkes County, only I hadn't bothered to listen till the blue lights come on.

The trooper who stopped had to have been in on it. He had a sniffer dog with him which scratched right away on the trunk lid, and two bricks of marijuana were under the spare tire. The way he found it so fast, the cop had to be in on setting me up.

I've done all but six months of the time they give me. Laying it out here at the county jail is better than the reformatory at Pendleton. Patty can come to see me twice a month and there's no way she could get here that often if I was any further north. I've stopped worrying about her leaving, so long as she don't find out Mary Parton was in the car I followed across the Ohio River.

I reckon things will work out.

Back home they still ain't cutting timber, but there's talk of men going back to work sometime this year or next. Every now and then I dream about being back in the woods with a chainsaw.

In the dream I'm cutting on a great high white oak, and I don't know which way it wants to fall. I'm standing there watching the chain eat into the tree, and I'm wondering which way the tree's gonna go.

Mary Parton's behind me. I feel her looking at me, and I wonder which way I'll fall this time.

That's when I wake up.

SYMBIOSIS

Eileen Kidd watched Harlan Carter wheel himself up a redwood ramp built for elderly or handicapped tourists. It was supposed to persuade them to stop at her place in Collier's Grove, rather than go on to fast food places near the state park. Harlan sold things off three tables Eileen let him set up beside the café. He's the only person Eileen's ever seen use the ramp.

At the counter Harlan sipped from the cup Eileen filled with coffee, then rotated his wheelchair toward Freddy Taylor. "Would it be right to say Rodney Stevens is symbiotic with us?" After carefully enunciating each syllable of "sim-bye-oh-*tick*," Harlan waited expectantly. Eileen wondered where he'd found another big word.

Her nephew Freddy ignored Harlan. So did the four state police detectives sitting in a booth by the windows. The cops were all looking outside, studying the town as though the quiet of an April morning might be prelude to something more interesting. There wasn't much to see beyond the plate glass.

Two young maples shaded Harlan Carter's ratty inventory. A few yards past the tables piled with junk, highway U.S. 60 ran east to Endicott Caverns State Park. It was the primary traffic artery for tourists who wanted to see more of eastern Kentucky than billboards on I-64.

"So. Is it right, saying that about Rodney?"

"Ain't nothing right about Rodney Stevens." Sliding off the stool Freddy slapped two quarters onto the counter and glared at the policemen in their booth. "Preachers say Jesus died for our sins. I reckon Rodney can go to Eddyville Penitentiary over them."

Having found nothing of interest outside their window, the detectives shifted their stares to Freddy, and looked wistfully at the door when he left the café. The policemen—and everybody else in Collier's Grove—knew Freddy was off to work fields of what was called "that stuff" in Hawkes County.

On the few flat acres of a flint-ribbed hillside farm Freddy grew an annual and legal three and a half tons of burley tobacco, worth thirteen thousand and change at auction. He had a brand new double wide, a satellite dish for television, and his four-wheel-drive Ford truck wasn't a year old. Seven thousand pounds of burley didn't make payments on all that, let alone support a wife with three kids.

"What do *you* think, Eileen?" Harlan raised his eyes to the café's owner. "Is Rodney sim-bye-oh-*tick* to us?"

Eileen didn't answer. Instead she wiped her counter with a damp towel and watched the policemen.

Harlan shrugged and rolled to the side door. An army-issue camouflage cap rode low on his head. Implying his legs had been lost in a Southeast Asian jungle, instead of a Chevrolet truck rammed into a tree, was good for his business.

The detectives didn't bother looking at Harlan. The first few days they were in town they'd spent considerable time examining his wares. They'd bought him quarts of coffee and provided an endless chain of free cigarettes before realizing Harlan wasn't going to answer any of their questions.

The screen door slapped shut and the policemen twisted their way out of the booth. Three went outside to wait by a grey government sedan; the fourth paused at the cash register. "We might stop by the county jail in Midland," he said while Eileen punched numbers. "Got any messages for Rodney?"

Eileen made change from a twenty and scrawled a receipt for the meals. She didn't answer, didn't raise her eyes.

"My boss says you'll be subpoenaed to testify at the trial." The detective left three one dollar bills on the counter, a big tip as such things were measured in the café.

Eileen put down her ballpoint and shoved the receipt across the counter. Her mouth was thin line in a worn face. "I won't do it."

96

"They'll put a subpoena on you." The detective put a toothpick between his lips. "They can *make* you come to court."

"They can make me come to a courtroom." Ashes from the Camel in her mouth dropped to the floor, but Eileen ignored them. "They can't make me say word one when I get there."

"What if a jury decides to fry poor old Rodney?" The detective's smile was a mean grimace. "You going to come to the prison and watch?"

"They don't electrocute retarded people." Eileen ran her towel across the counter again. "Jack Dillon dead wasn't worth this. Even for what he was telling you all."

"Who says he was telling us anything?"

Eileen's laugh was a sharp, humorless bark. "Jack wasn't the first to learn a hard lesson, telling other peoples' business. Nor likely the last."

The detective flashed the grimace-smile again as he turned toward the door.

No one spoke until the State men started their car and pulled onto U.S. 60, moving against an eastbound stream of motor homes and vans with canoes strapped to their roofs.

Alfred Hardy, old enough to boast the only Republican he ever voted for was named Hoover, prospected for change in his worn overalls. After a successful dig he put a pair of dimes and five pennies beside his coffee cup. "Gimme half a one a them honey buns, Eileen."

She lay the cellophane encased pastry in front of the old man. "You can owe me for the other half, Alf."

The old man peeled cellophane back and dipped one corner of the roll in his cup. Eileen tuned out Alf's tale of Vernon Fisher wrecking a new Studebaker truck one rainy night in 1953. She was about to spread her copy of the morning paper from Lexington when the telephone by the cash register rang.

Eileen wasn't surprised to hear Freddy Taylor's voice. Her nephew had come to the café to argue, but the presence of the detectives had kept him quiet. "I've about decided I'm going to talk to the state police," Freddy said. "Rodney Stevens didn't have no more to do with shooting Jack Dillon than I did."

"Where are you calling from?" Eileen looked over her shoulder toward the customers, though there was no one near enough to hear Freddy's voice.

"I'm . . ." He paused. "I got a phone in the truck now. I'm working. You know where?"

Eileen nodded, though Freddy couldn't see the acknowledgment. "Don't call till we talk. Will you do that?"

The telephone line crackled static for a moment. "It's not right what happened."

"They tell me radios can pick up talk from car phones," Eileen said. "Don't talk to nobody and I'll see you in a few minutes."

Dropping the phone in its cradle, Eileen looked at Alf Hardy and two other old men drinking coffee. Telling them the café was closed for a while wouldn't hurt her income; the old timers didn't spend much and the noon crowd wouldn't begin showing for another two hours. But Alf was still talking about Vernon Fisher's wreck, and none of the old men had anywhere else to go. Sighing, Eileen made another brief call before taking her purse from under the counter and going outside.

Harlan Carter's tables had attracted the attention of a blue haired matron who was carefully examining his stock of old dishes. The man waiting for her hadn't bothered to get out of the car, a white Oldsmobile with Ohio tags. "I've got to go see about something," Eileen said. "Susie Adams is coming to watch the place while I'm gone." Harlan nodded but didn't take his eyes off the blue haired lady. "And I need to borrow your van."

Burning Harlan's gas would compensate for the certain raid on her kitchen that would follow the departure of the Ohio car. The van rode higher than Eileen's Honda, useful where she was going. Hand controls were mounted on the steering column of Harlan's rusty Econoline, but the pedals worked too. Eileen waited for a break in traffic and pulled out behind a car towing a camper trailer.

The café was at the western edge of two mostly empty commercial blocks that were Collier's Grove. Eileen was in a hurry, but made a left on Railroad Street and circled twice before turning east on Main. Freddy would be livid if she allowed someone to follow her.

Driving out of town Eileen wished he'd go ahead and write the history of Hawkes County he was always talking about. As a boy Freddy was always scribbling something. If he started stringing words together again, maybe he'd write his way out of what he was doing.

He'd come home two semesters shy of a Berea College English degree. Freddy said he wouldn't stay longer than it took to save the rest of his tuition, but within three months Dotty Wagner was carrying his baby. Freddy bought the old Davis place and married her.

Eileen never had figured out who discovered the sandy soil where burley tobacco thrived would yield prime grade marijuana. Word spread fast, in any case. A year or two after Eileen first heard about it, marijuana was a major factor in the economy of Hawkes County. She didn't know a soul who smoked the stuff, but could name a dozen who cultivated it.

She steered Harlan Carter's van off U.S. 60 onto a gravel lane leading into the Daniel Boone National Forest and watched the rear-view mirrors. Satisfied she was alone, Eileen left the lane at a dirt road intersection and made two other turns before parking behind Freddy's truck. If the law caught her nephew growing marijuana on his own land, government agents would seize the entire farm. Freddy coaxed his illegal crop from public ground.

Freddy's engine was running, and the windows were closed. Eileen could see her nephew talking on his telephone. After a moment he put the receiver down and got out. "You know who Rodney Stevens' lawyer is going to be?"

"Who were you talking to?"

"Dotty."

Eileen didn't like Freddy's wife, a jealous woman who tracked her husband's every move when he was away from their house. "You didn't call?"

"Not yet." Freddy leaned against the bed of his pickup and studied the sky. "You know who's supposed to take care of Rodney in court? Linville Caudill."

"He's the public defender. That's what he does."

"Linville knows how to plea bargain drunk drivers. They're charging Rodney with *murder*." Freddy flipped his cigarette onto the ground angrily, and after a moment crushed it into the dirt with his boot. "Linville hasn't even asked anybody if they can alibi Rodney."

"It's only been three days."

"The day they found that pistol on Rodney and arrested him? I told two of those cops he was with me the night Jack Dillon got shot." Freddy shook his head. "You think those sons a bitches cared?"

"They knew you were lying."

He took a deep breath, and when he released it Freddy Taylor looked as though he might cry. "I wish I knew where he got that gun."

Eileen Kidd took a breath of her own, spoke in a sigh. "I gave it to him." She expected rage. Freddy only lit another cigarette and stared off into the trees.

"I was pretty sure it was you who told the cops Rodney had the gun," he said at last. "I figured the only way you'd know that was if you gave it to him."

"Those men from the state police weren't leaving until they arrested *somebody*."

Exhausted, feeling every one of her sixty two years like a dead weight across her shoulders, Eileen leaned against Harlan Carter's van. She wished she hadn't followed Freddy into the woods.

"Nobody cared if Jack Dillon lived or died." her nephew said. "Did you? Did anybody, except the cops he was snitching to?"

"Somebody cared enough you'd have gone to jail if Rodney didn't. They were watching you." Eileen felt as if she was baking in the heat, and wished she'd brought a cup of ice from the café. "If it wasn't you it would have been Terry Barker or Boyd Johnson.

Those detectives wouldn't care who it was, just so they took somebody to jail."

Freddy leaned forward to spit onto the ground between his feet. "They were looking for a killer. They didn't care about pot farmers."

"If I hadn't given them Rodney, they'd still be here," she said. "Another day or two they'd have been tired of eating my cooking and looking at Harlan's junk. They weren't going to leave without arresting somebody, didn't matter who. Or for what."

Freddy shook his head. "I don't know if I believe that."

Eileen looked at her watch. She'd been away from the café the better part of an hour, and had a noon meal to prepare. "I don't care what you believe," she told her nephew. Standing away from Harlan's van she wrapped fingers around the door handle and turned to look at Freddy again. "You and Dotty still coming to dinner Sunday?"

Freddy was watching the sky again. "I don't know," he said at last.

She nodded. "Call me when you decide. I need to know how much to cook."

"Wait." Freddy reached into the back of his truck for a hoe and a jug of water. It was a long thirsty walk to his distant fields. "Where'd *you* get that gun?"

Eileen shrugged and shook her head. "It don't matter where I got it. I had it though, and you're not in jail. That's the only thing I care about."

Eileen didn't cry until she was on the highway, pointed toward Collier's Grove.

OBLIGATION

Tom Frazier sits on his front porch and looks across the highway at the cluster of county vehicles crowding around Hubert Johnson's house trailer. The night is clear, the sky dusted with stars bright as new pin heads. Tom lifts his eyes, looking for the Milky Way, but the flashing red and blue lights in Hubert's yard make it impossible to see such faint luminescence.

Hubert Johnson was the last Hawkes County person Tom talked to, the summer morning in 1953 he left home. In a wet predawn fog Hubert pulled his pickup truck to the curb, where Tom stood outside Wilson's Drugstore, waiting for the bus that would carry him to Louisville. Cranking a window down, Hubert asked, "Been chasing the girls all night, Tommy? Need a ride home?"

Tom shook his head. "Not going home, Mr. Johnson," he said, feeling the self-consciousness of his grin. "Going to the Navy."

Hubert Johnson's eyebrows arched as he shut off the truck's engine. "Didn't think you was old enough for the service," he said, opening his door and joining Tom in the chill outside.

"Daddy signed for me to go."

"Ain't nobody coming to see you off?"

Tom shrugged and shook his head. It seemed more grown up to go away without an audience, and he hadn't been sure he could stand more wet-eyed looks from his mother. But time dragged miserably, waiting alone outside the drugstore.

"Got plenty of money?" Hubert asked. "I can lend you some if you need it."

Tom shook his head. "I got enough, Mr. Johnson."

Hubert stayed with him until the Trailways bus loomed out of the fog. Tom climbed aboard, and when he'd picked a seat, looked back outside. Hubert was still there, a big hand lifted awkwardly. Tom had never been further from his father's house than Ashland, and as the bus eased from the curb, he was glad he had Hubert Johnson to wave good-bye to.

The night is saturated with faint metallic chatter from two-way radios, and another squad car arrives hurriedly, as though squeezing one more official automobile into the tiny yard might right the wrong inside Hubert's trailer. Near the confusion of strobing emergency lights, highway traffic slows to a congested crawl, and Tom half expects to see an accident.

He shifts his gaze fifty yards east, where a high-roofed farm house is lit bright as Christmas. Mildred, Tom's wife, is there with Hubert's daughter Ruby. The ambulance that couldn't help Hubert is parked nearby, called minutes after Ruby ran screaming from the trailer.

Jesse Surratt, the sheriff of Hawkes County, stands outside the front door, talking to Ruby's husband. Tom is surprised when the sheriff gets in a squad car and drives away, toward town.

Tom has been waiting to be arrested.

In '84, when Tom retired from the Navy, he and Mildred looked for a house in Hawkes County. A pink-cheeked, enthusiastic real estate agent from Midland sent them to see the old Haggard place. Tom only half listened to the youngster's directions and declined an offer of a hand-drawn map.

He'd known the Haggards when they were more than memory in Hawkes County, thought he wouldn't need help finding the house. But east of town the highway expanded to four lanes, a concrete bridge spanned Three Doves Creek instead of a webbed steel one, and other landmarks were so altered Tom couldn't recognize them.

Passing the turn-off to Steven's Crossing, where the brickyard used to be, Tom knew he'd gone too far, and turned the car around. Lost, he pulled off the road where an old man sat in front of a mobile home.

"Deaf as a post, I bet," Tom muttered to Mildred, and left the car. "Excuse me," he said, raising his voice as he got closer to the old man. "I'm looking for the Haggard place."

"Nobody there," the old man said, puzzlement in his voice. "Haggards all left, better than a year ago."

"No, I'm thinking I might buy it," Tom explained. He looked up and down the road, recognizing nothing. "I grew up around here, but right now I'm lost as I've ever been in my life."

"Where abouts did you used to live?" the old man asked.

"Place called Head of Bearskin," Tom told him, and held out his hand. "I'm Tom Frazier."

The old man's handshake was cold and limp, and he stared at Tom, eyes narrowing to slits. "Gene Frazier's boy?" Tom nodded, and the old man grinned. "Didn't know me, did you, Tommy?"

Tom thinks someone must have recognized the pistol the old man used. The sheriff or Ruby *had* to have known who left it there. He's afraid of what will happen, once people—especially the sheriff—find time to think about the pistol. His hand trembles, lifting the second bourbon and water he's sipped since Mildred left.

He would leave the pistol again, if it were to do over.

He wishes Mildred would come home with news of what they're saying at Ruby's.

Rufus, the big male cat who lives in the barn, peeks around a corner of the house. Mildred won't tolerate him on the porch, and Rufus waits to make certain Tom is alone before coming ahead to leap heavily onto his lap. "Kind of a mess, ain't it?" Tom says, scratching around the cat's nicked and chewed ears.

When they stopped to ask for directions, Tom and Mildred were less than a hundred yards from the Haggard place. Hubert told them where the new turn-off was, directed them across a wide empty place where railroad tracks once ran, and they found the house half hidden in high weeds.

A V.A. loan inspector had already approved the house. Distracted, Tom didn't pay much attention, only strolled through the rooms, following Mildred. He found it hard to think about anything but Hubert Johnson.

The old man's skin had been icy as they shook hands, even in summer heat, and his clothes hung on him loosely, as though nothing of substance lay under the fabric. Yet there'd been a time when Hubert Johnson seemed the biggest, strongest man in Hawkes county.

Mildred bustled around the house, testing water taps, flipping light switches and examining each room closely before announcing her readiness to see the real estate agent again. Once in the car she launched herself into a monologue about the pros and cons of buying the Haggard place. Tom only half listened and drove without speaking. He knew Mildred was only thinking out loud and didn't expect him to say anything.

He was remembering when Hubert Johnson's general store, in the valley called Bearskin, supplied sixty or so families with everything from sugar to kerosene. Tom went to the store every day, to flirt with Ruby and be teased by grown-ups for his awkward attentiveness to the girl. Saturdays a truck always came from Midland to restock the store.

"You know what I saw Hubert Johnson do one time?" he asked Mildred as they passed a sign marking Midland's city limits. "I watched him take a fifty-pound bag of flour in each hand, lean over to pick up a twenty-five-pound sack of sugar with his teeth and walk off a truck like he was carrying air."

Tom let himself slip into the memory, recalling the crowd of grown men, most of them surely dead now, that watched Hubert Johnson's labor. "Tobe Foster said 'Jesus God, that man works like a mule.' Roger Adams was standing there with us, and he said 'Not exactly. You got to *make* a mule work that way. Hubert *likes* it.'" Tom laughed.

Mildred lit a cigarette with the car lighter. "We turn left at the next corner," she said. Lowering her window an inch she added thoughtfully, "Tell that young man we'll pay thirty thousand. Not a dime more."

Tom sees a hearse from the Rockwell Funeral Home back up to the trailer. Soon the police cars are gone, and the lights at Ruby's wink off. Hubert's trailer is empty, dark, and quiet.

Mildred comes home when Tom is halfway through his third drink. As she stops at the porch steps Rufus springs from Tom's lap to hide in darkness. "You *knew* what that old man would do," Mildred accuses, a quaver in her voice, eyes shiny as the dewy grass under her feet.

She stares at Tom as if daring him to speak. "What'd Jesse Surratt say?" he asks at last. "Is he going to arrest me?"

Mildred doesn't answer, and when she goes in the house, slams the door behind her. Through an open window Tom hears her angry steps slap across the wood floor in the hall. After a twenty minute stretch of silence, Tom tosses melting ice into the grass and follows Mildred inside.

He creeps with intoxicated caution into the bedroom, undresses and slides under the covers without touching his wife. Tom stares into the dark, wishing he could make her understand why he *had* to carry the pistol to Hubert.

After he and Mildred moved into the Haggard place, three or four times a week Tom found time to stop at Hubert's trailer. The old man called him "Tommy," as though he still saw the boy who went off in a fog to boot camp, and talked about long-gone people and places in a way that made them real again. Whenever Tom sat with Hubert Johnson, some fine days came close enough to touch.

A stroke nearly killed Hubert. He was in a nursing home for two months, in Midland. Tom visited him there, but couldn't bear to go more than once. There was no way, in that sad, camphored decay, to touch anything good.

When the doctors said it was all right to move him, Ruby brought Hubert to her house. She meant to sell the trailer, but her father wouldn't sign the papers. He spent his days gazing across Ruby's neat yard at what had been his home.

Grudgingly, Ruby relented and moved him back to the mobile home. Medicare provided a nurse for the better part of every day, and Tom sat with him daily from four o'clock until six, when Ruby brought supper for her father.

A constant dribble of saliva ran from a corner of Hubert's mouth, and his speech was only grunts and sibilant whispers.

One day Tom carried the old man outside, propped him in a chair in late afternoon sunshine. The sting of tears and his blurred vision caught Tom by surprise. An unbidden, vivid image swam up from some reservoir of memory: hulking Hubert Johnson flinging giggling children through the air and then catching them, Hubert laughing loud as any of them. Tom was one of the children, and remembered the reckless soaring sensation, just before the belly lurch of a stone heavy fall that ended safely in Hubert's big hands.

It wasn't right, Hubert Johnson turned into an old man who peed his pants, who drooled like an infant and had to be carried out of his own house.

In time Hubert's speech improved marginally, or perhaps Tom only learned to interpret what sounds he could make. Understanding the noises was frightening. When they were alone, the old man said things like "I lived too long, Tommy. They should've let me die in that home, instead of hauling me back like a broken old pet."

Another day, Tom told stories of places he'd been in the Navy: Barcelona, Naples, Tokyo, and Subic Bay. "Where would you go if you could travel, Mr. Johnson?" he asked.

The old man lifted a trembly hand to point toward the blacktop a few yards away. "In the road," he said.

Tom sat for a long time without speaking, watching the trucks roar by. He never mentioned travel to Hubert again.

And one morning, Hubert begged, "Lend me a pistol, Tommy. Help me out of this."

Tom never told Ruby or Mildred what the old man said when they were alone. But a week later he took the loaded magnum to Hubert, who watched Tom put it in a drawer by the bed, before Ruby brought supper. As he left a few minutes later, Tom was sure the old man smiled.

Tom stares blindly at the ceiling for a long time. Mildred's arm falls across his chest, and he feels her breath, warm on his cheek. "Ruby thinks you left Hubert the gun so he wouldn't be afraid, staying by himself at night," his wife whispers. "She thinks it was an accident, that it went off while he was trying to put it away. Don't worry about the sheriff."

Tom sighs loudly in the night, and as Mildred moves closer, he begins to cry. "It'll be all right," she says.

TROOPS

My name's Don Reynolds and I live here in Linden. I'm making this tape with the Veteran's Administration Troop Sightings Project, and I'm supposed to say I know I'm under oath.

I'm a contractor, commercial stuff mostly. I build fast food restaurants, that kind of thing. I'm married and have two kids. My Troop showed up the morning of July twentieth, waiting by the truck when I went outside to drive to work. He was from the Dominican Republic.

I was a Third Class Boatswain's Mate in the Navy, '64 to '69. When the government put Marines into Dom Rep in '65, I drove an assault boat until we landed all the grunts off a transport. Then the jarheads sent word back to the ship they needed truck drivers, and my division officer sent me and a bunch of other guys ashore to help out.

I earned a Troop the day I drove a platoon of Marines into an old part of Santo Domingo. The grunts were doing a house-to-house search for someone or something, and I was leaning against my truck, having a smoke, hoping they'd get done before dark. Those streets were a mean place once the sun went down.

It was over real fast. I saw somebody raise up, silhouetted on a roof, aiming a rifle at Marines a block away. He didn't see me or my M-14, and after he pitched off the roof into the street I didn't see him again. I was sure he was dead though.

So.

I knew who my Troop was, when he showed up. I figured he was about sixteen years old, but in Dom Rep people always seemed to be older or a lot younger than they looked.

Rumors said if I could see *mine*, I'd see everybody else's too. I thought about going back in the house and staying there for as long as it took him to go away. But the same rumors said Troops never went away. After staring at the kid for a while I got in the truck.

The passenger door didn't open, but when I turned the ignition key he was at the other end of the seat, rubbernecking like the streets of Linden were exotic and unbelievable. After where he came from, maybe where he'd been for nineteen years, I suppose they were.

There was a bad moment when I got to the new 7-Eleven my crew was building. Louie Knapp, the nearest thing Linden has to a town drunk, was slouched on a pile of lumber, not asleep but not real alert either. He had a brown bagged jug of Mad Dog pinched in one hand.

At least a dozen North Korean and Chinese soldiers clustered around him.

It was spooky enough, having a skinny Latino kid riding shotgun in my truck. The sight of a dozen Communist infantrymen from 1950 made my knees shake. While I was unloading my tools, Louie got up and ambled off toward Eileen Murphy's café, and his personal squad followed along behind.

There'd be plenty of room at Eileen's. Troops don't take up much space, and a thousand of them wouldn't make a crowd. It's hard to explain if you haven't seen Troops, and if you have, you don't need an explanation.

Eddie Taylor showed up and helped me restring the extension cords and air hoses we lock up at night so they don't finance Louie Knapp's wine. Eddie was pouty and pissed, and had been for days. Before Troops showed up Eddie had lots of war stories, but hadn't said much for a few weeks. He didn't have anybody trailing after him either.

The kid from the Dominican Republic followed me around while we got the cords and hoses down, not getting in the way, just *there*. I thought about the things people were saying about Troops.

No one's sure when the first ones got here. The psych unit at the hospital where my wife's a ward clerk had been full for weeks. Before he hung himself in the basement of the hospital, an old guy named Jerome Higgins wrote a suicide note about seeing them for over a year.

Higgins got a Medal of Honor at Iwo Jima, where he killed thirty-eight Japanese soldiers in one afternoon.

There had been a few scandals. Two Senators and a Governor who built political careers on war records resigned without explaining why. Joe Foster told me after Troops got to be common those guys were walking around like Lonesome Eddie Taylor, not a dead man in sight.

Joe's worked for me since retiring from what he calls "The Crotch." God help anyone else who makes fun of the Marine Corps around him. He was in the Big Green Machine twenty seven years, and the first time I saw Joe after my Troop showed up, I counted nine following him, including two Arabs.

The most interesting Troop trailing Joe was a white guy, a second lieutenant with Ivy League arrogance engraved on his face. The lieutenant looked insulted about having to stand around a not quite 7-Eleven while a couple of old enlisted men drove nails.

During our coffee break Joe caught me staring at the lieutenant. "Drifty motherfucker damn near got a whole platoon of us killed in sixty-nine," he told me.

I remembered an ensign named Yoder who called an air strike in on some grunts in '65. Yoder was in a hurry and got the coordinates wrong. He didn't come back from Dom Rep, and I wondered if Yo-yo Yoder was trailing another ex-Marine someplace.

"Anybody bothering you about him?" I asked.

"There's lots of second looeys following retired gunnery sergeants." Joe grinned, but not like anything was funny, and nodded toward my Troop. "Dom Rep?"

"Yeah." I looked at the kid who'd stayed close all morning and wondered if he could hear us talking. "Do they go ever away? Like at night?"

"You won't get much sleep for a while." Joe looked at my Troop again. "I was at Dom Rep. I figured I'd have two or three from down there, but except for the Arabs mine are all from Nam." He showed that nothing's-funny grin again. "I must've shot blanks all over that island."

Having the Troops with us wasn't that bad. Like I said, they never make a crowd, and only me and Joe could see them. After a while we pretty much ignored them like everybody else. And the Troops didn't pay much attention to us either.

Except for Joe's Arabs.

They watched like they wanted to help out, especially when me and Joe were installing cabinets and could have used like three hands apiece. I think those guys were carpenters before Joe killed them. They studied us the way I'd watch a builder, if I wasn't allowed to pick up a hammer myself.

When I got home, I watched the news with my wife, listened to Connie Chung talk about mass hallucinations in Bosnia. The hills around Sarajevo were crowded, and there was video of shaking and crying Serb gunners who'd killed uncounted numbers of men, women and children. Ruth couldn't see those same men, women and children clustered around the Serbs, but I could.

It was a quiet night at home, Ruth in her chair, me in mine. Marcie, our twelve year old was at gymnastics, and our boy Donnie was out putting mileage on his new driver's license. My Troop sat on the sofa and looked at the TV, same as Ruth and me.

"I think they're real," my wife said when Connie Chung started talking about something else. "Those ghosts or whatever they're supposed to be." Nobody was calling them Troops yet. That came about a week later, from a *New York Times* editorial. "What they say about mass hallucinations can't explain all that talk."

"You don't see him, do you?" I looked at the kid from the Dominican Republic while I asked the question.

Ruth put down the magazine she was reading. "*You* see one of them? One of those ghosts?"

"It doesn't seem like a ghost," I told her. "It's just a kid who won't go away."

I'd never told Ruth about the Dominican Republic. But while the TV advertised something for headaches I let her in on what happened down there. Then I went outside, snagging a six pack of beer from the refrigerator along the way.

I sprawled in a lawn chair and got shit faced, while my Troop squatted in the grass and watched a soccer game a bunch of kids were playing across the street. The Troop looked like he knew a lot about soccer.

"You play that game back home?" The kid looked at me when I spoke, but not for long. "You call it football down there, right?" This time he didn't take his eyes off the ball.

When the six pack was gone I lurched down to Kelley's Tavern and had a beer, standing up, eating peanuts. I asked for a six pack to go after Troy Johnson started singing "Hail, hail the gang's all here," waving a bottle over the head of a little Asian girl who wasn't worried about being carded. Troy was half singing, half shrieking "What the hell do *we* care, what the hell do *we* care" when I left.

Before I drank myself into a stupor on the patio, Donnie came home. I tried to get Donnie and the kid from Dom Rep to talk to each other. They were about the same age, but Donnie couldn't see the Troop and the Troop didn't seem interested in my son.

When Ruth woke me to go to bed I leaned on her, getting into the house. I swear it seemed like the Troop was holding me up too. When I had my shoes off and was stretched out he stood at the foot of the bed, very quiet in the dark. "Breathe, goddamn it!" I yelled at him after a while. It would have been better if he'd made even that much sound.

Ruth got tired of my babbling and mostly slept on the couch the first couple of weeks, until I got used to having my Troop around all the time. It was hell on our sex life though, all the time he was here.

I drank a lot of beer before it struck me becoming an alcoholic wouldn't help the situation any. Louie Knapp's Koreans didn't seem to be bothered by his Mad Dog. After that I drank like before, a few after work on payday.

The *Times* ran their editorial, and everybody stopped talking about hallucinations and got serious about figuring out what the hell was going on. When the Veteran's Administration started the Troop Sightings Project I called the 800 number like they asked us to. Nobody came to see me until today, but Joe and anyone else who reported multiple Troops got interviewed right away.

Joe spent a day at a V.A. lab, wired to machines. He recognized a lie detector and the EEG. They didn't find anything unusual. Joe didn't tell them about the lieutenant, and the only lab tech he saw with Troops winked and didn't say nothing either.

Louie Knapp killed himself before the V.A. got around to talking to him.

So did Troy Johnson.

So did a lot of other guys, and not just Stateside. Troops were happening all over the world. For a while it was nothing but dead guys on the TV news. The networks sent cameramen to Southeast Asia, and I hear they got miles of videotape someplace that was meant to settle that "missing in action" stuff.

But before anybody could study the footage the Troops went away, and now nobody knows what's really on all that tape.

I was so used to having the kid around I didn't notice he was gone until I got in the truck one morning and didn't have anybody riding with me for the first time in seven, almost eight months. By then we were building the Burger King over on Highway 62, and Joe Foster was late that morning. Taking a shower by himself was such a luxury he stayed in until all the hot water was gone.

Now I'm like everybody else, wondering if it meant anything. Donnie stopped talking about an R.O.T.C. scholarship to college, so some things *have* changed.

TV evangelists are having a great time talking about what the Troops meant, but preachers are like everybody else. They haven't got a clue.

Last night Connie Chung said it's been eleven months since one army fired on another, the longest period of peace documented since the world's *had* armies. Everybody's talking about the "Peace Age," that kind of thing.

Maybe that's what it is.

Joe Foster doesn't think so.

After work last Friday we put our checks in the bank and stopped at Kelley's. About the time we got our third beer Joe started talking about Troops. He says armies have to do what they know *how* to do, and that's kill each other. And he pointed out that with all this Peace Age talk going on, not one military unit has been disbanded.

Joe's worried.

"Sooner or later they'll start shooting again," he said. "And I got a feeling . . ." Joe took a big drink of beer before explaining. "You know how we used to send a fleet close to a country for a warning before we launched bombers and blew hell out of somebody's real estate? I think that's what the Troops were, a warning."

Joe says if they come back, they'll come back pissed. He's worried.

I been thinking about it.

I'm worried too.

JESSE'S BECKY

W hen the sheriff called to say the digging would start by early afternoon, Joe Sawyer went to the nearest bootlegger in dry Hawkes County and bought a case of beer. He's sitting on Jesse's porch, feet propped on a filled ice chest, sorry he promised his family he'd be there for the sheriff's search. Joe wishes the day was over.

The dissonant whine of a diesel engine, straining in the low gears, compels him to walk around the house. From the side yard Joe watches a truck's laborious climb up Jesse's hill road, towing a yellow tractor on a flatbed trailer. Reuben Foster, the county sheriff, follows in a police vehicle, red lights strobing, though there's no room for the truck to get out of his way.

Going back to his chair on the porch, Joe thinks the lights are unwarranted, resents the showy gesture. There's no emergency at Jesse's, just history.

The truck crests the hill and stops by the barn, where Reuben brakes long enough to let a woman leave his car. A pair of cameras are slung around her neck, and she begins taking pictures of the truck and the back-hoe tractor while the sheriff steers the county vehicle toward the house.

Reuben shows a toothy smile and calls "Good mornin,' Joe," as he and another man leave the squad car and come to stand by the porch. The sheriff's grin is offset by a chill in his eyes. "You want to come and watch?" he asks.

Joe shakes his head. "Too hot to stand outside, unless somebody's paying you to do it."

Reuben opens his mouth like he means to say more, but after a moment he walks away, leaving the man who followed him from the car.

"I'm Todd Clemens," the stranger says. After Joe has stood to shake hands, the man shows him a press card from a Louisville paper.

"You're a ways from home," Joe tells him, settling back in his chair, resting his feet on the cooler of beer again.

"More interest in this than you might think," Clemens says, turning to watch the tractor back slowly off its trailer, tentative as a fat man descending a ladder. "Where will they start digging?"

"Up in the woods, by the creek I expect," Joe says. "Come on up out of the sun." Clemens climbs the porch steps and settles into a wood rocking chair. "Want a beer?" Joe lifts his shoes off the cooler and ice rattles as Clemens reaches inside.

"Think they'll find a body?" the reporter asks when he's opened a can.

Joe shrugs his shoulders. "If they look in the right place, they will. Jesse never lied that I know of."

"Why do you think he did it?" Clemens asks.

Joe picks up a manila envelope on the floor by his feet. "Reuben gave this back to me yesterday," he says. TAKE TO SHERIFF is scrawled across the envelope in what looks like red crayon. Joe rummages in the envelope, pulls out a small black and white photograph, and hands it to Clemens.

The fading image is of a lovely young woman, wearing men's trousers and a flannel shirt. She's seated on a tree stump big as a kitchen table, legs spread wide, looking defiantly happy as she smiles at the camera. Clemens turns the photograph over, but there's no writing on the back. "Who is she?" he asks.

"Rebecca Foley, I think." Joe reaches for the photograph and studies it intently, as though he might find something new there, if he looked hard and long enough. "Jesse was a logger in the thirties. This was probably taken when she came to visit him in a lumber camp. Anyway, if that's Rebecca Foley, she's what this is about."

"Any chance of talking to her?" Clemens asks.

Joe shakes his head. "She died. A long time ago."

The reporter puts a small tape recorder on a table between them. "You mind? It's easier than trying to remember everything."

Joe shrugs wordlessly.

"Tell me about Jesse," the reporter urges.

Joe crushes the empty can he's holding and reaches in the cooler for another. He snaps it open, drinks deeply and begins to remember. . . .

When I was growing up, Sawyers were common in Hawkes County as fleas on a rabbit, but by the middle sixties most of us had moved out, found better jobs up north. Jesse was my father's cousin, the only one who stayed. He lived rough as a barn rat, half-starving on a V.A. pension and a little bit of cash from a few acres of tobacco every year.

I keep thinking about things the family believed about him.

Up in Ohio we said things like, "Jesse sure loves Hawkes County. He'd starve to death down there before he'd leave Kentucky." And we told one another how admirable it was that Jesse managed to be so happy with so little, on his scrubby patch of farm.

It never occurred to us maybe Jesse *couldn't* leave.

After the army I came back to Hawkes County to go to Midland College, and spent considerable time with Jesse. He knew—and would tell—family secrets, and I liked hearing my parents and aunts and uncles had been young and foolish once upon a time. He repeated old scandals, told me who was pregnant when they got married, who'd been in jail and for what, all sorts of things nobody else in the family ever mentioned.

I guess Jesse saved the best scandal for last.

About the time he turned seventy, Jesse fell asleep a few times, driving his pick up. After he steered himself off a hill, I became a sort of chauffeur for him. Jesse bought another truck, but if he wanted to go farther than ten miles from home, I did the driving.

I was down for a weekend last fall, and Jesse said some things that made me remember a day I'd almost forgotten, one of the times we went to a trade day over in Briggs County. Trade days were a chance for old timers to get together, swap anything from knives to shotguns, and pass pint bottles of bourbon back and forth.

Nobody knew old roads in Hawkes County better than Jesse, and he liked to go places along routes only he could keep straight. I was steering us down a two lane blacktop, wondering how in the world we were going to find Briggs County by driving west, when Jesse hollered, "Stop!"

I stood on the brakes, hard enough to pitch us both toward the windshield. I turned to see what was wrong, and Jesse was staring at a house.

On a back road lined with wood shacks and mobile homes, the building was out of place as an Arab in Sunday school. It was two stories, paint peeling off tall white pillars that would have done Tara proud. "What's a house like that doing out here in the middle of nowhere?" I asked Jesse.

"Two brothers, Teddy and Willard Jennings, ran a bootleg joint here, years ago," he told me. "It was a regular showplace." Jesse leaned out of the window to spit. "And a whorehouse. After a while, nobody bought whiskey anyplace else. They come a long way just to look at the women who worked for the Jennings."

"Sounds like you had a glass or two there yourself," I teased. I thought Jesse would grin with me, but he sat over on his side of the truck cab and stared at the house, seeing something I couldn't. He didn't seem in a hurry to move on, so I pulled the pickup onto the shoulder and switched the ignition off.

The house was enclosed by rusty barbed wire, and a couple of abandoned bales of hay on the front porch were a sign the house was someone's barn now. "Want to go inside?" I asked.

The old man stared at the house, eyes big as quarters, hand knuckled white around the pistol he pulled from under the front seat. Jesse always had the revolver with him, but no one ever thought much about it. He shot copperheads and rattlesnakes on his farm every summer, and everyone figured the gun was for snakes, or maybe groundhogs foolish enough to be seen in his bean patch.

We didn't know near as much as we thought we did about Jesse's pistol.

Jesse sighed loudly, like a man using breath to keep pain at a distance. A hard expression settled on his face as he nodded and got out of the car.

He brought the pistol with him. "Think we'll see a snake?" I asked, but he ignored my question. His arm hung slack, the gun dangling at his side. His knuckles were still white.

We stepped over the sagging wire fence, and Jesse paused on the porch. Looking up I saw a series of cast iron hooks twisted into the ceiling. "Some woman has kept a mess of plants hanging out here," I guessed.

Jesse shook his head. "Used to be four or five swings hanging on this porch," he said. "In summer, there'd be fifteen or twenty people out here of an evening, all about half drunk. If the women weren't busy they'd come outside too," he said. Looking at Jesse, I had the feeling the nights he remembered on that porch had been uncommonly fine.

"Want to look inside?" I asked, when Jesse continued to stare at the hooks, as though mesmerized by memory. "Trade day won't start for another hour."

Jesse shifted his gaze to the front door, took another deep breath and muttered, "Hell. We got time."

In what had been a living room, a rough table was set under an unshaded light bulb, and dozens of wooden stakes leaned in the corners. "Looks like somebody strips their tobacco here," I said.

Jesse drifted deeper into the house, floating like a leaf caught in slow, muddy current. I trailed after him, until he stopped at a closed door. Jesse turned the knob and shoved, but it wouldn't budge. "Open it," he said, the first words he'd spoken since we came inside.

I put my shoulder on the wood and pushed. There was a cracking sound, and I expected the door to break rather than swing on the rusty hinges, but it gapped far enough for us to step inside. Cardboard boxes lined the walls, and the room smelled of abandonment and dust.

"Them walls used to be the prettiest peach color," Jesse said from the threshold, his voice soft and dream-like.

"How come you remember the color of the walls?" I asked.

Jesse shrugged. "This was Becky Foley's room," he told me. "Her bed was by the window, and she kept a dresser, with a big mirror, over against that wall. Becky loved to set and brush her hair." The hand that wasn't filled with pistol moved to point to different parts of the room, but Jesse's eyes weren't focussed on anything at all. "Used to brush it for her, sometimes. Never done that for another woman in my life."

He was quiet for a long time before he added, "Becky died in here."

"Who was she?" I asked. Jesse had never mentioned her name before.

"A woman who stayed with the Jennings," was all Jesse answered. "It was Teddy Jennings' fault she died. After Teddy left out, Willard said Becky wasn't nothing but a bitch that got what she deserved." Jesse's eyes were wet when he turned away.

Too young to understand new tears for a death that was fifty or more years gone, I watched Jesse as he turned away and started for the front door.

I was glad to leave.

Driving to Briggs County, I tried to get Jesse to tell me more about the woman whose name made him weep. "She was someone I knew, and Teddy Jennings got jealous," was all he'd tell me.

"Did Teddy Jennings kill her?" I asked.

Jesse shrugged his shoulders. "Same as."

"What do you mean, 'same as'?" When Jesse wouldn't answer, I asked another question. "Where did Teddy go when he ran?"

"Nobody ever knew." Jesse looked down at the gun he was still holding, then slipped it under the seat. "Before we even buried Becky, Willard went to find his brother. He said there wasn't but three or four places he could run to, but Teddy wasn't anyplace Willard looked. Willard wrote a letter to one of his whores, said he was coming back to Hawkes County. We never seen him again, though. There was talk he got shot at a card game over to West Virginia, but nobody knows if that's true or not."

The rest of the time I was in college, I drove for Jesse at least twice a week, but he never offered another word about Rebecca Foley. The few times I said the name out loud, he looked away and didn't talk again until I changed the subject.

We never drove down the road where the house was again. By the time I graduated from college and went back to Ohio, I'd forgotten it.

Like I said before, last October I came back to Hawkes County and stayed with Jesse a few days. One night we drove to the top of a high hill, built a fire against the chill and listened as fox hounds bayed through the valley below us.

Jesse talked for a while about dogs he'd owned, and told me he'd dreamt of being in a dark hole with no way to climb out. He believed the dream meant he'd die soon.

Jesse had been part of my life as far back as I had memory. I tried to imagine him gone and couldn't.

"Ain't but one thing I'm sorry I didn't get done," he said after a while. "I wish I'd hunted down Willard Jennings and killed him when I had the chance."

The name Jennings was blank sound until Jesse reminded me of the day we walked through the abandoned house where Becky Foley had lived. "My God, Jesse, what are you talking about, wanting to kill somebody?" I asked, shocked.

"I meant to shoot him on sight, if he ever come back to Hawkes County," Jesse said. "If Willard was to walk up this mountain tonight I'd kill him, for saying Becky Foley deserved to die." While he was talking Jesse took his old pistol out of wherever he carried it, and stared at the weapon like it had let him down.

It didn't seem right, a man saying his own death was close, and talking in almost the same breath about a wish to murder. Before people die you expect them to let old grudges go. I wanted Jesse to explain, but he'd said all he was going to.

I went back to Ohio not long after that night on the hill. When Jesse was taken to the hospital again, I came back as soon as I could, but he'd already slipped into a coma. Last week we buried him where he'd told us to, in the old family cemetery on Caney Ridge.

I didn't come with the others to go through Jesse's things. My brother told me the envelope was on the kitchen table, out in the open, where no one could miss seeing it. When they carried Jesse to the hospital that last time, he knew he wasn't coming home again.

Todd Clemens finishes his beer and asks, "Any more in that cooler?"

"Help yourself," Joe says.

The reporter prods, "And that was how you found out about the rest of it?"

Joe nods. "There was a letter that said we'd find a body buried at the foot of an oak tree, near the fork of Three Doves Creek. Jesse said he didn't mean for there to be trouble if it was found later on.

"The letter explained what happened. Rebecca Foley was pregnant with a baby she swore was Jesse's. He came to get her, but Teddy Jennings wouldn't let her go. Becky told Jesse to go home, she'd be there by morning. Teddy made her drink something that was supposed to make her lose the baby. Whatever it was, it killed her.

"When Teddy heard Jesse was looking for him, he tried to run, but Jesse found him before he was out of Hawkes County. Teddy was buried on this farm before the sun set.

"That's why Jesse never left Hawkes County. If he sold the farm, someone might find the man he killed. And he'd have killed again, if Willard Jennings had come back."

Clemens reaches to shut off the tape recorder. "People like reading about someone who gets away with murder," he says. "I suppose I should go see if they've found anything." He pockets the recorder and stands up.

Joe reaches for another beer as the reporter steps off the porch. He holds the can without opening it for a while, gazing at the picture of the girl on the tree stump. Looking around the scrub farm that was an old man's jail, Joe doesn't think Jesse got away with anything.

He snaps open the can and listens. If he finds something, Reuben Foster is likely to yell, or make some sort of noise. Joe drinks off a third of the beer before he looks back at Becky Foley's picture.

Three Towsacks of Grapefruit:
A Kentucky Memory of The Great Depression

Abide Coldiron, feeling cold and brittle as the frost rimed grass beyond the porch, paused one step outside the door. In the distance, a young crow called across the Appalachian ridges, impatient for more daylight, and Bide shivered his sympathy.

Paul, his youngest son, waited at the barn, the mare mule Frieda already hitched to the wagon. Frieda pawed impatiently with her right forefoot, tail switching nervously, as though haunted by the memory of summer's biting flies.

For the first time in sixty-two years and some-odd months of drawing breath, Bide felt like an old man. In the ungodly year of nineteen and thirty-seven, everything had turned upside down. He waved, signaling Paul to bring the wagon closer, and his son bounced leather on the mule's back. She came eagerly. Halfway to Midland, Frieda might balk, refuse to move for anything short of a fire built close enough to burn. For the moment, though, she was as eager to go as Bide was reluctant.

Bide climbed into the wagon seat and reached for a plug of tobacco in his coat pocket. He picked lint off the moist, fragrant block, shaved a piece loose with his pen knife and tongued it into position in his right cheek.

He put the knife away, and when he slipped the plug back inside his coat, left his hand in the warmth. Bracing both feet on the dashboard, he slouched in the seat and leaned backward. He would have been halfway comfortable, if he could have stopped thinking about their destination.

A half mile passed with no noise at all except for Frieda's rhythmic breath, muted ringing from harness metal and a nagging squeak from the off front wheel. It'd need greasing before they started home, Bide thought. Should have done it yesterday, but an old man couldn't remember everything.

"Cold," Paul said at last, his resentment of driving the mule to town beginning to thaw with the frost now that the sun was higher. He had argued in favor of hiking to the main road and catching a ride in Hubert Fannin's milk truck.

Secretly pleased he wouldn't have an altogether silent ride into town, Bide only shrugged. He leaned over the wagon to spit and sighed loudly, settling back again. "Figures a year like this one'd bring the devil's own kind of a winter."

"It's been a time," Paul agreed.

A flood had taken all Bide's crops, drowned his three meat heifers. His milk cow was worthless since swimming a day and a night to keep her nose above water. Even next year's seed was ruined when Three Doves Creek ran through Bide's barn for two days. People who lived along sluggish Three Doves still occasionally found crow-ravaged bodies, resting eight or ten feet off the ground in remote trees.

A space of time went by in silence while the series of calamities, a mere three months that had all but wiped him out, ran over and over in Bide's mind. He didn't want to think about it but the memories came again and again, the way his father once claimed "Goober Peas" played in his mind for days on end sometimes.

It was good marching music, Bide's father said, until the whole Union Army picked it up. For months it seemed he was never far from someone's enthusiastic bellow, *"Goodness how delicious, eating goober peas!"*

For years afterward the cursed lyrics came on their own, playing day after day inside the veteran's head. By the time Bide was born, nine years after the War, only whiskey could stop the damnable music Bide's father heard.

Bide wondered if whiskey would make his three-month run of memories stop their monotonous cycle. It might, but it would send Amanda off to her sister in Paintsville as well. She'd done it before.

When Bide married seventeen-year-old Amanda Warren, he got mumbling, shuffling drunk at their wedding. Amanda said if he ever did it again she'd leave him. Believing her, Bide was sober eight years, until he happened to be in Midland when news came of the 1918 Armistice. Somebody shoved a bottle at him and he didn't go home for two days.

Amanda and the children were already in Paintsville by then, and stayed six months. When she came back Amanda swore she'd leave again, and stay longer, if she ever smelled alcohol on Bide's breath. He didn't doubt her vow was still valid. Whiskey might offer an escape from his string of miserable misfortune, but it would cost him his wife.

Frieda balked at the post road, in need of direction. Midland was south, the saw mill and Thompson's grocery, frequent destinations for the wagon, to the north. Glancing left, Bide saw Paul had dozed off. It wasn't cold enough to make sleeping on an open wagon seat dangerous, and so early in the morning few trucks and cars were on the highway. Bide reached for the reins, meaning to let his son doze.

Paul stirred, roused by the change in the wagon's rhythm. He turned the mule toward town and sat a bit straighter in the seat.

The sun crested the ridges, grew to a warming golden circle, and Bide gratefully unbuttoned his coat, leaving his hands outside his pockets. Then he remembered their destination, the damned Roosevelt charity commodities depot at Midland, and didn't feel so grateful.

The New Deal had Hawkes County hypnotized. Sometimes Bide wondered if anyone else in the state remembered what his father and other old men said about Democrat treachery and Dixie rebels dividing the country. Roosevelt's commodities, his WPA, CCC and the rest of the alphabet charities kept folks from remembering Hawkes was a Republican county, had been since the troubled times of 1860.

Halfway down Big Perry, the only mountain in Hawkes County with a name, town was so close Bide could smell it, a stink of shame and humiliation in his nostrils.

"You got to do it, Bide," Amanda had said, two nights ago. "You *got* to."

Chair pulled close to the stove while he whittled a new wooden handle for Amanda's butcher knife, Bide nodded. "I know," he admitted. "But not yet."

"What do you mean, 'not yet?'" his wife snapped. "Another two weeks, we'll be out of everything."

Three Doves' bad temper had them eating the end of last year's canning instead of new crops, flood-ruined fields having yielded nothing to refill Amanda's mason jars. That they naturally shared with Paul and Muriel only emptied the cellar that much faster.

"I'll not go tomorrow," Bide said tiredly. "The day after."

He'd gone to Paul's the next day, and the boy agreed to go along. It seemed easier for Paul, somehow, or perhaps Amanda was right when she called Bide boar-hog stubborn. Half the county was on relief since the flood, but there was no comfort in the misfortunes of others. That dozens of acquaintances regularly made the galling trip to the Midland courthouse didn't make Bide's journey any less difficult.

At the foot of Big Perry Paul directed the wagon left, and when town came into sight Bide nudged his son with an elbow. "Step her up, Paul."

The youngster stared quizzically for a moment, but obediently slapped harness on the mule's back. Frieda agreeably increased her speed to a canter. Bide felt a little better, arriving as though on a hurried, prouder mission than that of beggar.

The courthouse square was empty, unlike Saturdays when Bide generally came to town. Then it was difficult to find an empty space for the wagon while they transacted business with storekeepers and learned whose behavior in Hawkes County was worth talking about.

Paul guided Frieda into a vacant lot by the courthouse, not bothering to set the brake before climbing down. She was a good mule, and wouldn't roam while they were gone, unless she got hungry. Then she might move a yard or two in search of sweeter grass.

Bide hadn't voiced to Amanda or Paul his doubts there was hay or feed enough to carry Frieda through the winter. It would be hard if he was forced to sell her.

To Bide's chagrin, when they went around the front of the public building, he found no one was trying to keep welfare a secret in Hawkes County. An enormous sign loomed over them:

COMMODITIES OFFICE
IN THE BASEMENT
HOURS: 8 TO 3, MON-FRI

The sign looked as though it had stood there a while. But Bide couldn't remember ever seeing the shameless scarlet lettering on a white enamel background.

He ground his teeth angrily when he noticed the supports straddled the sidewalk. They had to walk under the damned thing to reach the basement entry. Anyone watching would know exactly where he and Paul were going.

They were twelve or fifteen feet from the door when it swung open. Malcolm Breckinridge stepped outside, arms burdened with two large paper sacks. Malcolm was only three or four years younger than Bide, but the pair of tow-headed boys following were sons, not grandchildren. Malcolm and Flora Breckinridge were raising four late children, the pair of boys, and two girls apparently at home with their mother.

Malcolm didn't seem ashamed at being caught at the commodities office. "Afternoon, gents," he said brightly, grinning like they were meeting at church instead of outside a beggar's basement.

"If I'd've knowed we was all coming to town, Mr. Breckinridge, we could've rid in together," Paul said.

Malcolm shook his head. "Flora and me been staying with her sister," he explained. "Times like these, if people throw in with one another, it's a little easier, seems like."

Listening, Bide formed a wordless prayer in his mind: Dear God don't bring me to this, don't make me give up my own home, send me grinning through the streets, proclaiming the convenience of family charity.

"Guess what the little chaps has got?" Malcolm said.

Malcolm's sons were dragging large burlap bags. The least one stood shyly behind his father's legs, let go of his bag and didn't look at them. His brother though, came closer and bent to open the neck of his sack. "Grapefruits," he crowed.

The burlap bulged with yellow globes, big as a baby's head. "You can have all you can carry," Malcolm said. "They got lots. Everything else is on ration, but they'll let you have plenty grapefruits."

Bide sighed and looked away from the image of Malcolm Breckinridge giving guidance on begging. Impatient to get on with it, Bide nodded curtly. "Tell Flora Amanda'd love to see her come for a visit," he said, and stepped around the boys and their father.

On the other side of the door a short stairway carried them into cool basement air pungent with citrus. Three bare bulbs illuminated the hallway, at the end of which another white and red sign confirmed they'd found the right office.

Beyond the sign a young woman stood behind a high counter, hair yellow as the grapefruit stacked all around her, smiling a politician's grin. Bide was sure he'd never seen her before. "Good afternoon, gentlemen," she said. Her clipped accent confirmed she was a stranger. "May I see your cards?"

"Cards?" Bide responded.

"The blue card from the county clerk. It establishes you as a resident of Hawkes County."

"I'm here, ain't I?" Bide knew he was being rude, snapping at the woman, but he'd somehow expected he'd only have to show up and carry off the charity food, avoiding encounters with happy paupers like Malcolm Breckinridge.

"Missy, I've lived on Caney Ridge, man and boy, for sixty-two year." Bide made his voice gentler. The young outlander hadn't made the flood, even if she did work for people intent on turning the world upside down. "I reckon I'm as established a resident as you got."

Her smile broadened, became genuine. "I'm sure you are, sir, but you have to register with the county clerk first." She reached under the counter and withdrew two pieces of paper. "If you'll fill these out and take them upstairs I'm sure everything will be fine."

It took ten minutes to finish the form, leaning on the lady's counter, using her pencil. Bide had to set down his name, date and place of birth, his wife's name, number of people living with him and other things Bill Everett, Hawkes County Clerk, would know without having them written out. The blonde woman was friendly enough, but a hard glint in her blue eyes made Bide certain there was no arguing with the requirement for the form.

When he returned the borrowed pencil he was granted a second business-like smile. "Now, sir, if you take that to the County Clerk, I'll be able to help you as soon as he gives you your card."

Bide and Paul climbed to the office on the second floor of the courthouse, where the situation became very odd. There wasn't any problem at all with issuing Paul one of the necessary blue cards, but the Ferguson girl who was Bill Everett's assistant looked into a big bound volume, stared at Bide for a moment and said he'd have to come back when Mr. Everett was in the office.

"Where is he if he ain't here?" Bide asked. Misguided voters being foolish enough to elect a lazy man like Bill Everett County Clerk, it seemed reasonable to expect the walking sack of air to be where he was needed.

Allie Ferguson flushed pink and said she didn't know. "He had things to do. Didn't say when he'd be back." She gestured toward the hard bench stretching along the wall opposite her counter. "Y'all are more than welcome to wait."

Bide shook his head. "I'll come back." At the door he turned and told Allie, "If Bill comes in, you tell him I expect him to see me before he takes off again."

131

Allie nodded.

In the basement, as soon as she saw Paul's card, the yellow haired stranger piled her counter with corn meal, flour, unground coffee beans, cans labeled "BEEF," and then added two middling jars of honey. She gave Paul two large paper bags to put the groceries in for easier carrying.

When Paul had the sacks packed, she put two burlap bags beside them. "You're welcome to as many of those as you want to carry home," she said, nodding toward the piled grapefruit. "Another day or two and they'll start to rot anyway."

Paul looked at the heaped fruit doubtfully. "I never cared for them things," he said. "Thanks just the same."

Bide put a hand on his son's arm. "Take some. They'd be good for Muriel." Paul's wife was six months into pregnancy. When the youngster didn't move, Bide took the burlap bags to the yellow mounds and filled both himself.

Straightening, he was barely able to lift them, but eased through the door and into the hallway before resting his burden on the floor and dragging it to the stairs. He'd not let the blonde woman see he'd taken more than he could carry.

They put the grocery sacks, and the burlap bags in the wagon, and then Bide and Paul went back to the County Clerk's office. Allie Ferguson told them Bill Everett still wasn't back, so they went outside and sat on a bench near the front door. Bright sunshine beat down on them as the day lengthened toward afternoon. They'd have to head on home soon, whether they were finished at the County Clerk's office or not.

"Off wheel's got to be greased," Bide reminded Paul. "Take it over to Buchanan's, get it done while I'm waiting around here."

Paul nodded and from the bench Bide watched his son direct Frieda onto Main Street and turn her right, toward Floyd Buchanan's garage. Then he was alone, sitting on the bench that on a warm day would be the gathering place for a troop of old men. Bide could recall when Civil War veterans, Union men all, held court on the bench every Saturday.

Bide could remember when those old timers seemed old enough to be Moses' contemporaries, but some hadn't been as old as he was now.

Twenty minutes later he climbed the stairs to Everett's office again. The County Clerk was still out, and Bide called Allie Ferguson close. "I ain't got much more time to wait," he explained, not complaining, just wanting her to know if she could resolve whatever the problem was, he'd appreciate it.

"I'm sorry, Mr. Coldiron," she said. "I can't do a thing till Mr. Everett's here."

"Well what *is* the problem," he insisted. Bide found it hard to believe ignorant Bill Everett could add to what he and the Ferguson kid could do themselves.

Allie stared over his shoulder for a long moment, then blurted. "Taxes." The girl blushed and looked miserable as a new widow.

"I pay my taxes, honey," Bide told her gently, wishing he could somehow comfort her.

"I can't find the receipt," Allie stammered, plainly lying. "I can't do a thing unless I can find it."

He waited long enough to know Allie was going to cling to her story about a missing tax receipt, hanging onto it like a cat holds the tree a dog has put it up. Bide considered the puzzling dishonesty as he went back to the bench outside. He *did* pay his taxes, hoarding the bulk of whatever cash he and Amanda came by, to avoid the foreclosure fate of too many neighbors.

Malcolm Breckinridge had probably lost his farm for nonpayment of taxes. Land could be bought cheap, if a man had the stomach for taking another man's home. Bide couldn't imagine doing such a thing, but others weren't so reluctant to enlarge their holdings.

Bide sat on the bench and cut another bite of tobacco off his plug. He put it in his cheek, let it soften and fastened his coat against the breeze that was getting downright uncomfortable. Another fifteen minutes, he decided. Then he'd start home. He'd just have to come back alone in a day or two when both he and his mule had rested from what was not an easy trip.

Paul came back in a few minutes, bringing Roy Stiles with him, a no-account who generally had nothing more pressing to do than hang around Buchanan's. "Papa, Roy knows what the trouble with the clerk's office is."

Roy looked embarrassed, same as Allie Ferguson. "Tell me," Bide demanded when Roy only stared at the new WPA sidewalk, put in as soon as the flood receded from town.

"How you registered?" Roy asked.

"What do you mean? Registered for what?" Bide sat on the bench, half-guessing what Roy would say.

"For elections." Roy Stiles took a deep breath before blurting, "Nobody but a Democrat can get commodities, Mr. Coldiron. Everybody knows that"

Bide peered crossly at his son. Paul had expressed considerable admiration for Louisiana's Huey Long, before the senator was assassinated.

The boy nodded sheepishly. "I meant to vote for Mr. Long, whenever he got around to running for President. I know you don't like Roosevelt," Paul said, suddenly defiant. "But be damn if I ever vote for another Hoover."

"Well I be damn if I'll be in a party that puts a do-less man like Bill Everett in an office and don't even make him sit in it," Bide snapped.

He left the bench, anger carrying him all the way to where Frieda waited in a patch of high grass. But before he could pull himself up into the seat his rage was spent.

He thought about Amanda's eyes, if he went home empty-handed. She wouldn't send him back, not after he explained what they were going to make him do for a pile of grapefruits and a small bait of meal and flour. But Bide could see the look in her eyes.

He turned so swiftly he nearly ran into Paul, hurrying to catch up. "Wait here," Bide ordered. "I'll not be long."

It was easy, once he got back to the Clerk's office. Bill Everett still wasn't in, but when Bide explained to Allie he wanted to change his registration, the girl's eyes looked relieved and she fetched a big ledger. All it took was signing his name in a different column. When Allie said, "Mr. Coldiron, I'm sorry but . . ." Bide held up his hand.

"Ain't your doing," he said.

In the basement the blonde woman was about to lock her door, but she let Bide in the commodities office, and doled out the same load she'd issued Paul. "You come back and see us," she said brightly.

Bide only nodded.

He carried his groceries to the wagon, then went back for the single burlap sack of grapefruit he'd taken. He didn't speak until he and Paul were out of town. Mostly he thought about his father, and those old Republican men who had disappeared from the bench outside the court house.

"You take all three of them grapefruit sacks home with you," Bide said to Paul when they turned onto Big Perry Road. "Get Muriel to eat as many as she can stand."

What he was taking home was bitter enough, Bide thought. He didn't need grapefruit.

About the Author

Bob Sloan's commentaries, which air regularly on Kentucky Public Radio member stations, have been recognized with a Public Radio News Directors, Incorporated (PRNDI) award, and in 2001 National Public Radio's *Morning Edition* began featuring some of Bob's commentaries.

In 2000 Bob was the Gold Medallist in the essay division of the William Faulkner Creative Writing Competition, sponsored by the Faulkner Society of New Orleans.

Bob has published over fifty short stories in quarterlies like *Appalachian Heritage, Potpourri,* and *Buffalo Spree*; his poetry has appeared in *Wind, Kentucky Poetry Review, Misnomer* and others.

He's written and narrated three sixty-minute "audio books." *Aunt Ethel's Plumbing and Other Tales* contains some of his radio commentaries, as well as some poetry and an unabridged reading of one of his short stories. *Haunted Hills* is an hour of previously uncollected contemporary ghost tales, and *Stories I Never Told My Mother* are a bit racier (but no stronger than PG). He's also the co-author and narrator of *Valley of the Shadow,* a history of the Rowan County War, the bloodiest and least known of Kentucky's mountain feuds.

Bob majored in creative writing at Purdue University and now teaches creative writing workshops in Morehead, Kentucky. He is the third generation owner of a small farm east of town, where he and his wife Julie live with three big dogs and a number of cats.

Printed in the United States
1496400003B/375

9 781893 239210